TYRONE AND MYLES

A Novella

GUERNICA WORLD EDITIONS 84

ALBAN KOJIMA

TYRONE AND MYLES

A Novella

GUERNICA
World
EDITIONS

TORONTO—CHICAGO—BUFFALO—LANCASTER (U.K.)

2024

*Names, characters, businesses, places, events,
locales and incidents are either the products
of the author's imagination or used in a fictitious manner.
Any resemblance to actual person, living or dead,
or actual events is purely coincidental.*

Guernica Editions Founder: Antonio D'Alfonso

Michael Mirolla, editor
Cover and interior design: Errol F. Richardson

Guernica Editions Inc.
1241 Marble Rock Rd., Gananoque (ON), Canada K7G 2V4
2250 Military Road, Tonawanda, N.Y. 14150-6000 U.S.A.
www.guernicaeditions.com

Distributors:
Independent Publishers Group (IPG)
600 North Pulaski Road, Chicago IL 60624
University of Toronto Press Distribution (UTP)
5201 Dufferin Street, Toronto (ON), Canada M3H 5T8

First edition.
Printed in Canada.

Legal Deposit—Third Quarter
Library of Congress Catalog Card Number: 2024931001
Library and Archives Canada Cataloguing in Publication
Title: Tyrone & Myles : a novella / Alban Kojima.
Other titles: Tyrone and Myles
Names: Kojima, Alban, author.
Series: Guernica world editions (Series) ; 84.
Description: First edition. | Series statement: Guernica world editions ; 84
Identifiers: Canadiana (print) 20240289307 | Canadiana (ebook) 20240289323 | ISBN
9781771839204
(softcover) | ISBN 9781771839211 (EPUB)
Subjects: LCGFT: Novellas.
Classification: LCC PS3611.O485 T97 2024 | DDC 813/.6—dc23

For Jeffrey Tokazewski, M.D.,
who contributed a great deal to steering my literary creativity
toward
the birth of this novella

Hospital

A MASSIVE STROKE hit the left side of Tyrone's brain on the morning of May 7, 2012.

That morning Tyrone had a scheduled appointment with his doctor for a routine checkup. Myles had seated Tyrone in a portable wheelchair before they came down in the elevator.

Outside the apartment building, Myles parked Tyrone by a wooden bench by the glass entrance door. Leaving him there in the wheelchair, Myles ran out to the parking lot in front of the building, got into the sixteen-year-old Mercury Sable Myles had bought from Tyrone four months before when he had decided to stop driving because of his weakening right leg. Myles turned on the ignition.

Tyrone, with his head titling right and his jaw hanging and his right arm dangling over the arm of the wheelchair, thrust into Myles's side vision. Myles made an abrupt turn toward the entrance. He nearly hit a concrete pillar by the bench. Stopping the car halfway up on the flagstone floor, Myles dashed out to Tyrone.

Tyrone is dead! a voice screamed inside Myles's ears.

Myles ran into the foyer, snatched the phone from the receptionist and dialed 911.

No more than three minutes passed before Myles heard the siren. He shoved his hands under Tyrone's armpits and dragged his large body off the wheelchair before gently lying him on the flagstone. He was giving him a mouth-to-mouth resuscitation when a red ambulance turned its nose at the far corner of the premises and headed toward them, the siren explosive now. The vehicle had just come out of the garage at the Department of Fire and Emergency Services two blocks west of Route 70. The receptionist came out of the building to help Myles. One of the three medics was already holding Myles back away from Tyrone.

The medics at once placed Tyrone on the gurney they had pulled out of the vehicle and squeezed a thick spring-like plastic tube into Tyrone's mouth down into his chest. On reflex, Myles sucked in a huge amount of air, witnessing how easily this flexible tube disappeared into Tyrone's body. The medics raised the gurney with Tyrone on it, folded its legs with care, then pushed it into the vehicle. The ambulance was heading for Memorial Hospital. Myles hopped into his Mercury and followed the ambulance. The siren scattered all the cars on Route 70 West to the right edge of the highway.

Six doctors rushed into Emergency Room 8 in the hospital where Tyrone was waiting. The curtain was slightly open. Myles sat outside the room, against the wall across from the door. He heard the physicians' coats swishing against one another, their suppressed voices arguing in low pitches. Then:

"He's not responding!" Mechanical noise followed this desperate yet determined female cry.

Myles stood up. In the nurses' station diagonally across from ER-8, the head nurse stood up at the same time, came over to Myles, and grabbed his shoulders. "Mr. Odam, sit down, please. He will be okay—just needs a little time."

Myles glanced at the round clock on the wall in the nurse's office. It was eight after one.

The curtain opened and six physicians in white coats came out. The last physician closed the curtain and approached Myles.

"Your brother is fine," she said. "Let him rest now."

"Can I see him?"

"No. Not today."

"When can I see him?"

"Give him at least three to four days to recover."

"Thank you, Doctor—"

"Dr. Canon. I'll be your brother's physician while he stays here." She touched Myles's arm and then joined the rest of the physicians now entering a conference room west of the nurse's station.

⁂

As per Dr. Canon's suggestion, and despite his anxiety, Myles only returned to Memorial on the fifth day following Tyrone's admission. By that time Tyrone had been transferred from ER-08 to Room 612 in the Intensive Care Unit. Tyrone no longer was on the breathing machine, but he had thin pliable tubes in his nostrils with a cloth bandage securing the tube right above his upper lip. Myles stood enclosed in the door frame of Room 612 and remained there, watching Tyrone lying in his hospital bed covered with a sheet up to his neck. A thin gray shadow covered his left eye—it was open but dead, the still eye casting its blank stare at no point in space. His right eye, pensive, traveled left and right across the corner where the ceiling and the wall met. Tyrone did not see Myles. Myles said nothing. He had prepared what to say to his older brother when he visited him in the hospital, but all those words had escaped from his brain. The image of Tyrone, unconscious and flaccid and his mouth gasping for air, had stuck in his heart. It was the kind of image that had never previously existed in Myles's mental definition of Tyrone. Myles wanted this new image to go away, but it did not budge. Instead, it continued to occupy the center of his consciousness. It devastated Myles that the power of nature could defeat such a powerful man in a split second, abruptly transforming him into an invalid. Tyrone, Myles's fierce brother who occasionally allowed his gentle side to surface, had been diminished.

Tyrone's head turned to the door where Myles was standing. His right eye brightened, and his angular face softened. Both the corners of his mouth stretched. "Don't just stand there and stare at me, Myles." A smile came over Tyrone's face, and a set of large, perfectly aligned teeth shone between his lips.

Myles approached the visitor's chair by Tyrone's bed. He hesitated.

Tyrone's hand peeked out of his top sheet, and his index finger pointed at the chair.

"The nurse said you're doing pretty well," Myles said as he sat down, taking his time.

Tyrone's gaze focused on Myles's narrow forehead. "That was a stroke of luck." His voice had lost its volume, but it held its serenity and the baritone pitch Myles had known throughout his adult life. "My speech survived. Thank God for that," Tyrone said it as if to himself. He then repeated it.

"God?" Myles said, craning his neck.

Tyrone nodded, with a childlike innocence Myles had not seen for decades.

"I've never heard you say that before, brother."

"It comes to you—when you've faced death."

"I know you have." Myles sensed Tyrone's gaze directed at the side view of his face.

"Give me your hand, Myles." Tyrone held Myles's hand in the way he used to arm-wrestle with him; he gave it a feeble squeeze.

Myles chuckled, aware of how big Tyrone's hand was. Tyrone grew up big-boned and muscular, with large hands and feet. In contrast, Myles came into this world with a fragile physical frame. Myles, a weak and nervous boy, had always envied Tyrone's strength, even as he feared how Tyrone might use it during one of his violent mood swings.

Myles returned Tyrone's squeeze and, with his free hand, patted their two hands joined together. "Does that mean you're going back to church?"

"I wasn't thinking that when I thanked God for my speech a minute ago."

"I know."

"You've got a sneaky way of making fun of me, you know that?"

Myles smirked and undid his hand. "I wanted to ask you something."

"What?"

"You always resisted church—even when our mother insisted it."

"I don't know. I was, like—seven years old?"

"I was five—I remember. I didn't know what was going on. So, I just tagged along with mother."

"Something ... you know ... something made me dislike sitting in the pew, looking at the dead man on the cross, listening to Father—uh, what was his name? Uh ... anyway, listening to him preach. Even now I can't figure out what made me stay away from church."

"At fifty-three now, I can sort of guess."

"Guess what?"

"You were a born agnostic."

"What makes you say that?"

"As long as I remember, you never believed anything that wasn't backed up by facts—things you feel, see, hear. A doubting Thomas."

"Most scientists are like that, don't you agree?"

"I don't know. Some people like you study bacteriology, others study theology."

"I guess you're our theologian then?" Tyrone laughed softly.

"Maybe I'm not a good churchgoer, but it doesn't mean I'm an agnostic. I'm not an atheist either."

"Then what are you?"

"One who sees religion as not a real important part of life." Myles raised his eyebrows at Tyrone and nodded as if to say to him, *You should know that.*

"I guess that's a good way to be." With the help of a bar hanging from the ceiling, Tyrone shifted his body rightward.

Myles went around Tyrone's bed to the other side and squeezed two pillows under his side to support the new angle of his body. He covered Tyrone with his top sheet and the wrinkled hospital blanket, then he returned to the visitor's chair.

"Medication time, Mr. Odam." A nurse came in with a trayful of medical gadgets.

Myles stood up and moved the chair away from Tyrone's bed to make a room for the nurse to tend him.

After recording Tyrone's vitals on the chart that had been hanging at the foot of his bed, the nurse broke open nine seals that contained tablets and dropped them into a small plastic bag. She then picked up from the tray a device that resembled a large stapler. She placed and held the plastic bag with nine tablets against a square closure at the leftmost side of the device. She then pushed down the handle, her forearm muscle tightening. The device made a creak, and the tablets crushed. She repeated it five times. She mixed the crushed medicine with four ounces of water in a small container and let her syringe suck in all of it at once. The nurse removed Tyrone's sheet and blanket and exposed a hose dangling from his lower abdomen.

"What—" Words coagulated in Myles's throat.

"Oh, this?" The nurse realized what caused Myles to react in that way. "A J-tube—a feeding tube. It goes right into his intestine. Mr. Odam's swallowing muscles have been damaged by the stroke." She injected the medication mix into the tube and followed it with eight ounces of liquid nutrients. After cleaning the tube with an additional eight ounces of plain water, she covered the J-tube first with his hospital garment and then with his blanket and sheet. "Done." The nurse smiled at Tyrone, put the cups, the pill crusher, the water pitcher, and the empty can of nutrients neatly back on to the tray. She made her exit, her mind probably already on her next patient in the adjacent room.

"What's the matter? You and your blank face." Tyrone chuckled in a coarse pitch.

"You can't eat anything, Tyrone?" Myles whispered.

"For now, no. But you never know."

"Even water?"

"I can have water, but I can't drink it."

"What do you mean?"

"I use suction swab. Like, sucking water out of a sponge. I'll show you—open the drawer for me."

Myles opened the top drawer of the side table and saw a square green sponge with a long handle. As he held it, he took a good look at it. "You keep the sponge portion soaked in water, don't you?"

"Yeah, that's right. And I pull it out, suck the water from it—a little at a time, though."

Myles put the suction swab back in the drawer and sat down, leaning forward to face Tyrone, his elbows across his knees.

Neither spoke.

"Do you feel tired?" Myles asked.

Tyrone whispered: "Yeah."

"Get some sleep," Myles said, getting up and preparing to head out.

"What are you going to do?"

"I'll go home now. But I can come back later."

"But did you check the visiting hours?"

Myles did not hear Tyrone. The J-tube, the tube feeding, the sucking of water through the swab, a bar to lift himself—how bad would he be? His heart thudded at the thought that he might have to become Tyrone's permanent caregiver, nursing a brother whom he had not seen for nearly three decades. Chained to his care night and day? Certainly, sending Tyrone to a State nursing home could be one option. But could Myles dive into doing it? Not looking back, and unable to believe his reconciliatory visit from Indiana would turn into this, Myles headed for the elevator—chills going down his spine.

Rage

THE MOMENT HE got home, Myles grabbed a tall glass from the kitchen cupboard, filled the glass with tap water from the faucet, and gulped it down. He sighed and smacked his lips. He then rinsed the glass and put it upside down in the light beige plastic basket by the sink.

Myles wondered how long Tyrone had had this beige basket before he'd moved here from Mishawaka, Indiana. The color, light beige, did not match Tyrone's natural predisposition towards anger, quick elation, abrupt depression, and subsequent reticence. Myles thought he was more likely to opt for a square aluminum container with three or four narrow openings at the bottom to drain excess water. He opened the cupboard and saw the rest of the utensils were all colorless—clear glasses, white ceramic plates and cups, silver pots and pans with black handles. Maybe when Tyrone's wife had divorced him after eleven years of marriage, she had forgotten to take the beige basket with her, or Tyrone had kept it as a souvenir of his failed marriage. Myles had avoided the couple while their divorce process was underway.

Myles felt the beige basket with his fingers. It was not hard plastic but a thin steel covered with beige rubbery material. Myles imagined Tyrone throwing this basket as hard as he could in a fit of anger, but the basket would just bounce all over the place as if laughing at him, further stirring up Tyrone's anger. He wondered how often Tyrone had flown into a rage at his ex-wife, how many souvenir plates and treasured mugs he had thrown at her in uncontrolled fury before all he had left was this utilitarian life.

That was the brother Myles had grown up with. He was never sure when Tyrone might summon his anger, ready to explode. That uncertainty turned into fear the first time Tyrone physically attacked him.

❦

Myles had taken it for granted that the school he attended in Mishawaka, Indiana bore the name "Virgin Mary Elementary School." Years later,

Tyrone corrected him: "That little old school? *Blessed Mary School for Boys.*" He continued, "When you started at Blessed Mary in 1965, I was in third grade. I stayed there until I was seventeen, when I left Mishawaka for Philadelphia."

Back in Mishawaka, Myles and Tyrone had been like twins glued together at the hip. They walked to Blessed Mary together every morning; they sat together in the school's multipurpose room to have lunch; and they came home together. Every morning Myles quietly waited for the lunch hour, except when the teacher asked him questions in class. Some questions, Myles could not answer; but for those he could, Myles answered as few words as possible, for he was terrified of making mistakes and being laughed at by his classmates, who teased each other relentlessly. But they ignored him, as he was not an important contributor who could add fresh flavors to their conversations and activities. Myles was okay with just sitting at his desk, looking at his textbook, daydreaming.

It was obvious that Myles was Tyrone's brother, not just because they spent so much time together, but because they resembled each other so deeply. Myles was slender, but his face was a small version of Tyrone's. Other kids did not attempt to bully Myles—they were afraid of Tyrone who had grown large for a twelve-year-old. He was the tallest kid in his class with his legs as big as tree trunks. The physical education teacher and some of the fathers of Tyrone's classmates thought Tyrone would make a great football player in a few years when he would be a high-school freshman. But, despite all this expectation, Tyrone played no sports. Myles would sometimes overhear kids whispering about it.

Going home, Tyrone and Myles sometimes went by a roundabout way through the woods behind the school properties to munch on wild berries, hazelnuts, and pine seeds. Other times they collected insects in the deserted field nearby the woods. Tyrone, after his science teacher had dissected a small frog to show the class what was inside this little creature, became obsessed with the frog anatomy. Myles lost count of the frogs Tyrone had caught in the field and ripped open to see their pink lungs jump right out of their bodies. Then he would pinch the frog's left eye with his fingers and pressure the eyeball out of its socket.

He would then ask, "Gee, so big. It's looking at me. Do you think he can really see me now?"

After his anatomical investigation, he would eat their well-muscled thighs and spit out the tiny bones.

"Here, try it." On Tyrone's open palm was a near transparent frog leg, skinned and cut at the trunk joint.

"No." The smell of bloody raw meat forced Myles back two steps.

"It tastes like chicken."

"You cook it for me first—then I'll believe it tastes like chicken."

"You're the chicken." Tyrone smirked at Myles and brought his mouth to the frog on his hand.

Myles snatched at the frog leg in Tyrone's hand and threw it in his mouth. It hit the ceiling of his throat. Myles's mouth filled with a horrifying bloody taste. He stopped breathing in the hope of stopping the taste. His fingers pinned a thin piece of bone sticking out of the meat and pulled it out of his mouth while his front teeth abraded the meat off the bone. Myles bit on the meat. And he chewed on it.

"Not bad." These words surprised Myles.

"Good. Next time, let's hunt some frogs for our dinners."

"But we're going to cook them," Myles looked at him in the eye, standing with his legs apart like a soldier.

"Done deal."

From that day on, every time Tyrone mentioned their frog hunt, Myles wrinkled his nose, twisted his lips, and shook his head. The deal never materialized. Myles enjoyed the sense of victory over Tyrone.

Myles sought Tyrone's company because Tyrone was always around, always accessible—not because Myles looked up to him. For his part, Tyrone might like it when Myles would follow him like his royal dog. If Myles were not within his sight, Tyrone would look for Myles the way protective parents might. In later years, Myles guessed their mother had told Tyrone to watch him because he hardly spoke—as if he had a learning disability. Myles simply did not respond to people readily.

But Myles did not have any learning disability. He learned vocabulary from reading, and Tyrone was a great help, often reading to Myles especially before his little brother started attending Blessed Mary. Myles was conditioned to see his brother as his protector.

One afternoon Myles and Tyrone arrived home from school together—Tyrone led the way walking faster than usual as if to tease Myles. Myles struggled to keep up with his brother, who sped up the walkway to the house. Tyrone strode through the doorway while Myles trailed behind him. Myles saw Tyrone slam his left shoulder square into the heavy wooden doorframe. Tyrone grabbed his left shoulder with his right hand, fell into the foyer, and crouched. Myles ran up behind him and removed his hand gently. Some blood had seeped through his creased white shirt. It looked like he had punctured his shoulder on a loose nail. Myles had never heard Tyrone blurt out such a fitful moan. Myles ran to the bathroom and soaked a hand towel with cold water, wringed it hard once, and, with his white bathrobe, took the wet towel to Tyrone. More blood had oozed out of the wound. Myles managed to pry the shirt off Tyrone's large frame and placed the towel over the cut. He pulled the string off the robe and tied the towel onto his shoulder with it. Tyrone kept panting but seemed to catch his breath.

"What happened?"

"You saw what happened, Myles. I bumped into the doorway."

"Something's wrong with you," Myles whispered.

"If there is, it's got nothing to do with you."

"What if it happens again?"

"What make you think it will?"

"You've been bumping into some other things lately, all on your left side."

Myles's heart thudded twice, hitting the ceiling of his skull. He was not sure if he should say it to Tyrone's face. It was too late—Myles's lips already articulated what had been on his mind for months. "Your left eye, Tyrone. You can't see out of it so well anymore. That's why you stay away from sports, right?"

Tyrone pushed Myles off him, and stood up, staring at Myles.

Myles stepped back.

Tyrone stepped forward. His right fist cracked Myles's jaw.

Myles flew a few yards and landed on the floor, hitting his head against a corner of the side-table by the couch.

"What are you saying!"

The boys' mother called out from her bedroom nearby. "Now what's all that racket out there?" Her voice was like a white canvas.

"Ma, go back to bed!" Tyrone yelled. "You've got no business here."

"Don't, Ty—" Myles tried to interrupt.

"I'm getting out of here. I'm going to Auntie Jo's."

Tyrone snatched his dark green bookbag, tossed it over his right shoulder, and dashed out. A furious bang of the door shook the entire house.

"Cecilia!" Myles heard his grandmother yell from her room upstairs. "Tell those boys of yours to stop slamming doors in my house!"

Myles crawled to a narrow space between the couch and the side table, rubbing his jaw, unable to cry.

☙

Tyrone's fury, which Myles witnessed for the first time that day, signaled there was more to him than being Myles's protector. A ten-year-old could sense things intimidating, things drastically wrong. But he was too young to reason why and how such things would happen. Myles listened to the whisper of his gut—to stay away from Tyrone. With his strength Tyrone could have crippled Myles, or even killed him.

Despite their closeness, Tyrone rarely interacted with Myles physically. He never hugged him, or his mother or even Grandmother Cora. They themselves rarely expressed physical affection for these children either. Cora was always busy with chores, and their mother seemed oblivious of them unless she had something to say. Then she was back into her oblivion.

Cecilia, their mother, sometimes hugged Myles, but only when he went to her with his arms open—which was rare. Her hugs touched his back, with the lightness of a feather. When he grew a few years older, Myles surmised that his silence had kept her at a distance. As far as Myles could remember, the truth was that he feared everybody around him. The townspeople of Mishawaka seemed to speak with strange voices with ever changing facial expressions: large stern eyes, thin lips, mouths with uneven silver teeth, toothless mouths, square jaws. Some of them voiced gently, smiling with twinkles in their eyes, ruffling their hair. But he sensed no goodwill behind these voices and faces. This fear had occupied a large part of his brain and had built a fortress of its own to begin its long years of residence inside.

Townspeople were not his only intimidators. Myles dreaded Grandmother Cora, who ruled their house ruthlessly. Her hexagonal face with high cheek bones scared him. Her eyebrows were missing, with her eyes slanting upward. A sharp straight nose nearly touched her upper lip, with her nostrils flaring sideway. She never looked up at anyone straight. The kitchen and the concrete laundry tub outside the kitchen were two places where she busied herself with chores that never seemed to end.

Cecilia liked sitting in the porch watching freight trains run east and west threading their ways through the trees in the woods that separated their backyard from the railroad track. In summer Cora kept the porch windows open. In winter she left snow and icicles that had piled up at the windowsills untouched—she knew Cecilia would like to look outside through the snow-covered windows. The mosquito screen inside the windows stayed there throughout the year, blurring the weeds in the backyard.

Cora always prepared the two boys' breakfast and dinner. Myles could not remember their mother ever doing that for them. When the food was ready, Cora would yell: "Kids!" Her voice had no inviting ring to it. Cora would not join the boys at the table. She took her food upstairs to her bedroom, where she would sew, knit, listen to the radio and sleep for the few hours when she wasn't working. Sometimes Cecilia sat with the boys at the kitchen table, but she did not stay there long. Maybe the opaqueness of the kitchen and the rotten-sweet odor of garbage emanating from a tin-can by the sink depressed her. From the ceiling suspended a naked dim bulb that blinked at irregular intervals. The boys often took their food and milk to the porch to eat. The sun brightened the porch. The air coming through the mosquito screen cleansed the food, Myles felt. The food smelled fresh.

The day Tyrone socked Myles on the jaw, Myles did not join Cecilia for dinner in the porch. He stayed in the narrow space by the couch. It was late spring, but the sense of season had left Myles—his body turned cold. He folded his knees against his chest and braced them with his arms. His eyes were shut. The darkness in the living room pricked his skin. He did not know how long it had been since Tyrone dashed out of the house. The night had fallen, and the house remained darker than the night.

In this darkness, Myles had a weird sensation that someone was watching him. Myles wished he had his blanket: it would cover him from head to toe, cutting off his view—he would not have to face the darkness staring at him.

Just then the air in the living room made a subtle move. It at once fell still. Myles raised his eyes toward the kitchen. Was it Myles's imagination? Or did he see someone who was not there?

"It's me, Tyrone."

"Don't. Please don't." Myles crawled backward against the wall. "I'll keep my mouth shut. Stay there, please."

"Auntie Jo sent me back home." Tyrone was coming toward Myles. Tiny black floaters spread across Myles's vision in the darkness.

"I'm sorry I clobbered you. It just happened."

Myles started to cry and felt dizzy. But he did not faint.

Tyrone unloaded his bookbag from his shoulder, put it on the floor, and sat on his heels in front of Myles. Tyrone opened the bag and said: "Auntie Jo was afraid you wouldn't be eating. She wrapped a couple of leftover turkey sandwiches for you." Tyrone pulled out of his bookbag two triangular sandwiches wrapped in waxed paper.

They were thicker than any sandwich Myles had ever had. The mixed smell of the turkey meat and homemade mayonnaise whet his appetite.

"Here, eat. I'll bring some milk for you." Tyrone put both the sandwiches on the side table and switched the lamp on. He then went to the kitchen, stopping for a moment at the doorway, touching the left frame of the door to keep his balance.

Myles picked up one of the sandwiches and peeled the waxed paper off the bread. He smelled his Aunt Josephine's hand lotion on the paper.

Deliveries

"Excuse me. Where is my brother?" Myles asked a nurse with an unfamiliar face. "He was in Room 612."

"Mr. Odam was transferred to Progressive Unit on the second floor," the nurse said as she kept on typing. "His room is—" The ticking of the keyboard stopped. The nurse brought her face to the computer screen. "Room 220. Close to the elevator."

Myles at once trotted over to the elevator shaft. One of the doors opened, and he hopped in. The elevator floated downward with no sound, no vibration. He felt as if gravity was suddenly sucked away from it. A nauseous sensation arose in his empty stomach. As he got out of the elevator on the second floor, he dashed to the water fountain in front of the wall across from the elevator. The fountain water cooled his throat, and then it descended into his stomach. The water tasted good. With the back of his hand, he wiped his lips hard.

Tyrone was sitting up, leaning against the pillow on the raised bed. "Here he comes." His voice was hardly audible, but his face with a faint smile signaled to Myles that he was feeling better that day. And Myles was certain that the sunlight coming through a picture window would please him, also.

"You look good, brother." Myles sat in a visitor's chair that was slightly larger than the one he had used on the sixth floor.

"Comfortable?"

"When do you start your rehab?"

"Dr. Canon said in a day or two."

"Are you looking forward to it?"

"No. You know, I haven't walked since I was admitted."

"Are you afraid?"

"I don't know if the stroke affected my walking or not."

"What did the cardiologists say? Anything?"

"No." Tyrone seemed seeking something from Myles. "Not yet."

"Not yet?" Myles cast his sight beyond the picture window—a wide blue expanse without an ounce of cloud. "Maybe they have nothing else to tell you. Have you thought of that?"

"Maybe I can use a walker. Even better—an electric wheelchair."

Tyrone's positive outlook surprised Myles. Myles wondered if Tyrone already knew he would not walk again. Would Tyrone be on the couch in the living room for the rest of his life, like that young man with lung cancer who had lived in Mishawaka—the man Myles delivered food to every other day because he was too sick? James? Yes, that was how Myles remembered him, though he had never learned the young man's last name. "Tyrone, do you remember James?"

"James who?"

"The young man who lived in an old house all alone."

"What was his last name?"

"I don't know. I don't think he ever told me. He was sick, remember?"

"Oh, he had some kind of incurable disease?"

"Yeah, James. Auntie Jo and I used to deliver food to him."

"Oh, yeah. You took me to him, didn't you? He was nice and very alert—I remember now. We had a lively conversation. We drank Coca-Cola. They never let us have that at home. I wonder whatever happened to him."

"He's gone now, Tyrone. He's been gone a long time."

Tyrone let out a sigh. "A lot has been gone a long time." He turned and faced the window, and fell quiet.

⚜

It had all begun when Myles was eleven years old, when he stumbled on what he thought a brilliant idea for earning a hundred dollars to buy a blue bicycle. His Aunt Josephine at once became the center of his focus as a potential financial source. No sooner had this idea organized itself in his brain than Myles approached Josephine when she was on one of her two-day-a-week visits to the Brooks Street house where Myles and Tyrone lived with their mother and grandmother.

"It looks like you need some help, Auntie Jo?"

"From whom?"

"From me."

"What for?"

"For your church work—giving people free food every other day."

"Oh?" Curious, Josephine stopped watering a bonsai tree on Myles's table in the porch, turned around, and leaned against the handrail enclosing the porch. Myles sat in his hard chair at the table. "You've got something on your mind, my little Myles."

"Isn't it hard you have to take food to people in town, all by yourself, Auntie?"

"It's not easy," she said.

It had taken a monumental courage on Myles's part to get to this point but now he was stuck.

"Well, how can you help me?" Josephine was now facing him straight.

Myles's tongue froze in his mouth. Quickly, he looked toward Brooks Street—like his mother had done often.

"You must have some reason. You're a smart boy."

"I can go with you when you visit people, and I can carry the food for you. And—"

"And what?"

"And, it could be like a job for me?" Myles asked, not sure how to ask his aunt for money.

"Well, that's very industrious of you. And those people will love you, Myles."

At once fear loomed over him. Having to meet townspeople was not in his calculation. Now he was not sure if he wanted that bicycle after all. He looked for his cocoon.

"Let's do it." She came by Myles and stroked his back. "And I will pay you a dollar and a half an hour for your services."

Myles was stuck again. He wanted the money, but what about the townspeople? Names like "the mute from Brooks Street," "that poor Odam boy" rang inside his ears.

"Well, I've got sandwiches to make. We start tomorrow." She extended her right hand. "Deal?"

They shook hands. Myles felt his body shaking all over.

The next day, Myles hardly spoke to anyone—including Tyrone. Tyrone did not make a big deal of this as usual: He knew something was going on in Myles's little brain. Josephine might have already told Tyrone about their deal. Myles had been thinking of the delivery job all morning, trying to drown out his fear with calculations of his earnings. If the afternoon delivery took three hours all together, he would receive four dollars and fifty cents from Aunt Josephine. This was more than a good deal for Myles. But the townspeople ... how many of them would Myles have to meet?

"Ready, partner?"

"Yes, ma'am," Myles whispered, not looking at her.

"Okay. Hop in." She stood at the back of the car, looked over the packages, counting the ones stacked on the right side, and then shut the hatchback.

When Josephine stopped at the curbside of a white bungalow, a couple opened the entrance door and came outside, the man smiling and waving. The woman stayed inside, leaning on her walker.

"You brought your little one with you, Jo," the man said while eyeing the frozen food Myles was holding—all neatly wrapped and put in a plastic bag. Myles did not know whether to give it to the old man or to hand it to Josephine.

"We brought a hamburger dish, with coleslaw and some string beans for you two." Josephine took the covered tray from Myles and handed it to the old man.

"C'mon in. Jo and—"

"Myles. My younger nephew."

"Oh, Cecilia's boy. I remember holding you, Myles. You were the tiniest baby I had ever seen." He gazed at Myles from head to toe. "Nancy, come out here. Guess who's here. One of the Odam boys."

Nancy, while limping, descended the four stone-steps one at a time. "Oh, dear. You *are* Myles. Yes, you were so small. I used to be Cecilia's baby-sitter. You've grown up."

"He's eleven now. Still growing, and growing fast. He's a shy boy though."

Why all this? Myles thought. *Why can't we just leave the food to them and go on to the next house on the list? Is that all this town thinks of me— as a dwarf baby?*

"Why don't you two come inside and have some iced tea?" The man gestured them to come into the house. Nancy nodded in agreement, beaming to see Myles for the first time in years.

"Thanks, Thomas. We will have to take a rain check on that. We have more houses to visit."

"You've got a lot to deliver, I know."

"See you day after tomorrow."

Josephine and Myles jumped in the Volkswagen and U-turned in the direction they had come from.

Passing by Myles's house on Brooks Street, Myles glimpsed Cecilia in the porch, looking outside. Her gaze did not follow the Volkswagen. Cecilia's eyes could have been closed—there was no way of knowing what she was thinking if she was thinking anything at all.

They passed Josephine's church, turned westward on North Brooks Street, and crossed a bridge that divided Mishawaka into east and west sides. Josephine parked the car parallel to a house that stood by itself surrounded by an unmanicured field full of dead weeds. The house gave an impression of being deserted for years: The white paint on its exterior walls had peeled off, the windows had blackened with grease—nothing inside could be seen from outside. Two of the window frames had gotten loose. Myles immediately wondered if this family had a fireplace to burn firewood in the winter.

Myles's family had always had a potbelly stove in their living room. Tyrone had become the stove keeper of the house. Myles never knew where Tyrone had learned it, but he could ignite fire on some newspaper that Grandmother Cora had finished reading, and then spread that flame onto the firewood methodically. Tyrone could intensify the amount of heat the burning wood generated. Sometimes he would show up at regular intervals from nowhere in the house to stir and then pulverize the shimmering red wood that was on the verge of extinction. With a charcoal rake he'd make room in the stove and add two pieces of dry firewood. He got joy out of handling burning wood, generating the heat to warm the entire house. The house warmed fast because of its small size of one-and-half stories—Grandmother Cora had her room on the half of the second floor above the boys' room. Her room extended out into a rooftop sitting area.

Josephine and Myles got out of the Volkswagen.

"Number 7 please, Myles," she said.

Myles went around the car to the back, opened the hatch, picked up a pack with the marking "7" on the wrapper.

She knocked on the door of this battered house. When no one answered, she put her right ear against the door.

Myles waited behind her, holding the food pack, anxious what kind of person would live in this rickety house.

Just as soon as the door opened, the door got stuck on the wooden floor. It then opened further, grating.

"Josephine, how nice of you to stop by." The man seemed in his twenties: He had his long, brown hair neatly tied in ponytail—his gaunt face ashy. He wore an olive-gray button-down dress shirt tucked inside a pair of khaki pants with no belt. "Oh, I see you brought a helper with you." He leaned to the doorknob to see a better look at Myles.

"My nephew, Myles." She turned to Myles and said: "James's arms are too weak to receive the package. We have to go inside with him."

"Thank you, Myles. You can put it on the coffee table." The young man sat in his couch. Myles learned it much later that the South Bend Salvation Army had donated to him pieces of furniture when a social worker, through the report written by his pulmonologist, found out that this young man had no family, that he had no possessions of his own except a garbage bag full of good clothes he had kept. "Myles, you sit by me here on the couch. It is as hard as a piece of wood. But, still, it does its job." His sunken, wide eyes narrowed, and his lips parted. "Jo always sits in the armchair."

What a gentle face, Myles thought.

"So, James, what did your doctor say?"

"Three months."

Josephine's lips tightened. She shook her head. "And you are living in this old beat-up house?"

"Doc suggested a hospice—a good one in South Bend, he said. But I am comfortable with this house."

"You need care, James."

"It's by choice, Jo, that I am here. Doc makes house calls. This is one of his stops."

A beat-up house, a young man with no vitality, good clothes, and "three months"—Myles could grasp none of this. Yet as Myles listened to his crystal-clear speech sound flowing out of his lips, Myles could not help but unbolt his heart, mesmerized by this young man's purity and quiet fearlessness.

"Would you like to have your food warmed?" Josephine asked.

"No. That won't be necessary. Thank you."

"When you need anything, just call. You have my number."

"Jo, you have other needy people waiting for you. And your little partner." James sighed and turned to me.

Myles swallowed hard and rubbed the palms of his hands between his knees. He turned to Josephine.

"Okay then. We'll come back the day after tomorrow."

"God bless you, Jo. And your silent boy."

Did James sense Myles had a hard time speaking?

"You need a blanket?"

"No. I'm fine."

Josephine got up and walked over to James and gently kissed on his forehead.

James nodded.

"Get well soon," Myles managed to whisper. He was uncertain if James heard him or not. Myles's heart pounded so much louder than his voice—a voice that trembled and got stuck in the throat.

James extended his thin hand with long bony fingers. Myles shook hands with him.

Josephine ushered Myles out through the door. Something was whirling in Myles's chest. His eyes were welling hot. Myles turned around and took one last look at James's dilapidated house. Myles hopped into the Volkswagen.

It was almost six-thirty when Josephine and Myles finished their food delivery. Josephine gave him four one-dollar bills and two quarters for fourteen deliveries in three hours—the first job Myles had ever had. He thanked her, holding his head high. She ruffled his hair hard and said, "Congratulations, partner."

On the way home, Myles did some math: He earned four and half dollars today, but he had ninety-five dollars and fifty cents left to make—sixty-four more hours of delivery. He had a long way to go. Behind his eyes, that used Vintage 1960s AMF Roadmaster Junior Bike shone azure.

֍

By the end of 1970, James was supposed to have been died because of his pulmonary condition. When James first mentioned the word "pulmonary" to Josephine, Myles thought it meant something to do with the stomach. He consulted his school's Webster's English dictionary. The dictionary clarified for him that this word referred to the lungs. Myles then realized James had been suffering from lung disease—neither James nor Josephine had explained what type of lung disease he had. Myles did not ask, either.

When Josephine and Myles first started delivering food to James, James had no muscles—they had dissolved into nothing—only the bone structure remained. James was on a cane: He could not walk without it as he had lost his muscular strength. But his eyes always shone bright as if they were telling he was going to live ten more years. And his speech had never lost its clear articulation and its confident ring. Despite his pulmonary doctor's prognosis of three months, James was still alive in the spring of 1972.

It was a Sunday early afternoon that April when Myles stumbled on the idea of visiting James not as Josephine's helper but as a thirteen-year-old who had bought a bicycle on his own. The truth was that, in the back of his mind, Myles had a secret urge to show James his bicycle. Josephine and Tyrone had thrown some kind words about his accomplishment—but they were his family members. Myles also wanted to see him and try practicing how to talk. Myles did not think Josephine had told James about Myles's problem, but James knew it anyway—Myles remembered James calling him a "silent boy." Myles was reluctant to go alone, so he planned to get Tyrone to go with him. Tyrone would do most of the talking, Myles would then chime in bit by bit and gradually talk more.

"Tyrone," Myles asked.

"Don't bother me now." Lying on the floor on his stomach, Tyrone was glancing through a long brochure of some sort. He did not look up.

"I'm going to see James."

"Who's James?"

"He gets food from Auntie Jo's church three times a week."

"So?"

"You want to come with me?"

"To see someone I don't know?"

"You'll like him. He was real sick two years ago."

"Now he is jumping around?"

"He's getting better." Myles stepped inside the doorframe of the room and leaned against the wall. "Auntie Jo thinks it's a miracle."

"What is?"

"James's getting better."

"What, like some kind of Bible story?"

"If you don't want to go with me, that's all right."

Tyrone folded the brochure and threw it on his bed. It boomeranged halfway toward him. "Okay, Myles. Let's go."

Myles dashed out to get his bike that he had left by the kitchen entrance.

Tyrone came out of the house.

"Get on the back seat," he said and straddled over the front seat of the bicycle. The front seat looked awfully small, in proportion to Tyrone's body.

Myles locked his arms around Tyrone's waist. Myles never knew a bicycle could run so fast—Tyrone's legs seemed moving at a leisurely pace, but the bike ran forward with the speed akin to Josephine's Volkswagen when she drove it.

"Is this his house?" Tyrone's right eye scrutinized the single-story house that stood in the middle of a silver-grass field, its white paint peeling off and exposing dots of the wood grain beneath like sores on skin, and its doorway warped. Tyrone turned to Myles as if he found it unbelievable that anyone would live in this kind of shack.

Myles nodded. He then took the bike out of Tyrone's hands and laid against the wall by the door. Tyrone had not moved. He seemed transfixed by the condition of this house. Since he was born, Tyrone had never come around this area. He had never seen this house.

Tyrone and Myles stood facing the door. "You better push the door, Tyrone, because it's stuck at the bottom."

Tyrone placed his right shoulder against the door and pushed it in.

"James, it's me—Myles."

"The door is unlocked. Just come in." James's familiar voice rang.

Myles went in first. James was lying on the couch and reading the day's morning newspaper. "This is my brother, Tyrone."

James sat up, pushing his blanket behind, folding his newspaper. "Good to meet you, Tyrone. I apologize for not having anything much here in the house. Myles, could you bring a chair from the kitchen, for Tyrone?"

"Oh, no. I am fine just plunking down on the floor, sir."

"That's what Myles does when he stops by with Josephine." James chuckled. "By the way, just call me 'James'. Do they call you 'Ty'?"

"No. I've always been 'Tyrone.'"

"A good name. Do you two boys go to the same school? Mishawaka Public, or Blessed Mary?"

"Blessed Mary," Myles said.

"He's an eighth grader, and I'm in tenth." Tyrone took it over. "Myles has his bike, but we still walk to and from school, like we always did."

"I envy you guys. When you are the only child, you get all your parents' attention; but, you know, you have to pay the price—loneliness."

"You didn't have friends?" Myles asked.

"I was not good at making friends. Shy—you know."

He is like me, Myles's silent voice whispered.

"Auntie Jo told us you are getting better." Tyrone was looking straight at James.

James's smile shone with hope. "My doctor did mention a slim chance of getting better a long time ago. It's just that he is puzzled why it's happening now, not a year ago."

"What's happening, may I ask?" Tyrone's curiosity popped out of his mouth.

"It's called 'remission'."

Tyrone and Myles both threw blank faces at James.

"Okay, the remission means that the disease you have had for a long time disappears for some reason. You may feel well, but the disease may still be in your body—it's like hibernating."

"The disease will come back, then." Tyrone's curiosity, once again.

"Most likely. Maybe two years from now, maybe even ten years from now. We just don't know when."

Tyrone's gaze was fixed on James, his brain was turning quick, and he had some questions he wanted to ask but was hesitant if he should—his right eye was telling Myles all that.

"Would you care for some Coke?" James asked as if giving Tyrone a few seconds to select some questions out of many his brain was generating. "Myles, could you get three bottles from my refrigerator and three glasses for us?"

Myles dragged a side table and placed it between James on the couch and Tyrone on the floor. He then brought the cold Coca-Cola bottles and plastic cups James had asked for and put them on the side table. He then poured Coke into the three cups, Myles's hand holding the bottle trembling.

"Thank you," Tyrone said.

Whether Tyrone was thanking James or Myles, Myles was not sure. He sat on the floor across Tyrone. The ice-cold Coke traveled down his throat, spreading a glacial sensation across his chest. Myles put his cup on the side table, then picked it up again, and had two more sips.

Tyrone had not touched the Coke. He just gazed at the cup filled with the dark purple-black liquid that they never had at home. "Were you born here in Mishawaka?"

"I am from Chicago. Have you been to Chicago?"

"No. But I'd love to go. What kind of city is it?" Tyrone took a sip of Coke from his plastic cup and let out a sigh of satisfaction.

"Downtown is like New York made miniature. Much cleaner than New York. Many restaurants, great stores for shopping. Lake Michigan is my favorite. It's huge, like the ocean. I love the noise the water makes along the shoreline."

"Your parents live there?"

"They died when I was twenty-one." James picked up his Coke, looking into the dark liquid. "A car accident in New York City."

"I'm sorry, James. I didn't mean to probe." Tyrone trailed off.

"Not a problem, Tyrone."

"My teachers say I ask too many questions."

"That's a good thing. A good amount of curiosity leads to a deep level of questioning." James's ringing tone confused Myles now. He grasped nothing of what James had just said.

"My teachers mean that I am obnoxious. My questions annoy them."

"You are a challenger, Tyrone."

"I don't mean to be."

"Be who you are. No need to change."

"You are the first person who has said that to me."

"And what others have said to you?"

"Shut up and follow what everybody does. Don't be a troublemaker."

"I know what you are talking about. I was there, too."

"How did you overcome it?"

"By embracing who I was. This is the only way. It's a kind of self-discovery, you know."

James turned to Myles and said, "You're awfully quiet, Myles."

Hot prickling sensation flashed over Myles's face and spread across the back of his head. "Just listening." Myles was not sure if James heard him. It did not matter.

"If all goes well, James," Tyrone switched to lighthearted tone. "What are you going to do? Go back to work? What did you do before you came to Mishawaka?"

James grinned. "Let me answer you backward. I was a statistician for Rosen Insurance in downtown Chicago—for seven years. I won't go back there. My plan? I will be a full-time custodian for Father Evans's church. The Church of Blessed Mary. Your Aunt Josephine goes there." He took one mouthful of Coke and put the cup on the table. "What is your plan, either of you?"

"May be some kind of medical researcher," Tyrone said. His cup was empty.

"I don't know, now." Myles pushed his Coke bottle toward Tyrone.

Tyrone grabbed the bottle and filled his cup with Coke. He then pushed the bottle toward James.

"Thanks. I still have plenty here." James raised his cup. "You will be part of a research institution, like NIH?"

"Yeah."

"Go to college, get medical degrees."

"What's a custodian do?" Myles interjected.

"Oh, my job? I will be checking the building. I will collect trash. I will sweep the floors and clean the windows. I'm going to be busy."

When Tyrone and Myles straddled over the bicycle, James came to the door—with no cane. He waved at the boys.

"A good man," Myles said, waving back at James.

"But why the change—from a high paying job to a janitor? He could be a consultant," Tyrone said.

"Maybe he chose to be a church janitor."

The bicycle propelled forward as Tyrone pumped the pedals.

Maples

With a nurse supporting at his upper arm, Tyrone walked along a bar attached to the north wall of the hospital's rehabilitation room. Tyrone would touch the bar from time to time, but he maintained his straight posture.

Myles stepped into the rehabilitation room just as Tyrone was making a left at the west wall. Thus it was Tyrone's back with his broad shoulders and thick neck came into Myles's sight—and that elated him. Myles stood there and looked at Tyrone, smiling. The nurse was wheeling a portable oxygen tank with her left hand—just in case he might have trouble breathing, Myles reasoned. Myles did not miss the pliable tube Tyrone had jammed into his nostrils. Not wanting to divert Tyrone's concentration walking, Myles strode over to the bench covered with gray imitation leather. Above the bench stretched a wide window with no partitions, like the one in Room 220.

Myles sat down on the edge of the bench, his elbows resting on his knees, and his gaze following Tyrone and his nurse. Myles noted a name tag on the nurse's chest, which read: Ann Safian. She had a short but defined nose line, with shallow eye sockets and thin unpainted lips, and the jaw line that curved gently toward her chin. But he stopped pondering upon her features. The sun coming through the window, warming his neck and the back of his head, was much too pleasant to focus on anything. As long as Tyrone enjoyed her company, that was enough for Myles—for now.

Myles stood up and faced the seamless window. Outside stretched a meticulously manicured garden with no flowers but multi-shades of green—pale green to near purplish green, cream-green foliage to glossy deep green. In this green population of plants stood a row of six maple trees behind a long wooden bench where a woman with silver hair down to the middle of her back sat, just letting the gentle breeze caress it. She leaned forward on the tip of her cane with her hands, resting her chin on her hands. Her pale white face reflected the sun which gave her face a luminescent glow. Her profile reminded Myles of a marble bust.

Myles's gaze shifted to the maple trees behind the old woman. They were all Red Dragon Japanese maples. Myles knew their names, because a Red Dragon Japanese maple just like those had been growing in the backyard of his family home on Brooks Street. Just like the maple at home, each of these behind the bench spread its foliage sideways, like a butterfly. All six of them together, not pruned, formed a large canopy without any symmetrical shape, only their branches and foliage leaning forward over the bench. Myles could see Tyrone's appreciation for these beautiful maple trees.

Myles recalled, when they were teenagers, Tyrone would love the noise his bookbag made when he dropped it on the floor by his bed. He would then step over to the window, to look at the Red Dragon Japanese maple. This maple was the only thing that grew in their backyard—no flowers, no decorative stones, no bird feeders.

"Was it already there when you were little?" Myles asked Tyrone out of curiosity.

"The maple?"

"Yeah."

"Our grandfather planted it—that's what Grandmother Cora said. I wasn't born yet."

*

Nothing new happened at their foster home—Josephine's house. Myles did miss his big brother roaming about in their shared room. Myles missed Tyrone standing at the old window—sometimes over an hour, looking at the Red Dragon Maple tree in the backyard. In those moments, Tyrone must have been pondering why he was born with no sight in his left eye, why his mother had neglected him despite he being her first born. Maybe Tyrone had not been her first born— he could have been her third or fourth. Those whom she had before Tyrone might have been stillborn, or they might have been given away for adoption. Myles never heard their mother saying she loved Tyrone. Nor did Myles ever recall him bringing up that he loved her. Myles suspected that there was no love lost between them. If anything, Myles speculated, the family court judge's verdict for the kids to move in with Josephine lightened Tyrone's burden—his burden of having to share the same roof with a mother who did not, or could not, retain the memory of giving birth to Tyrone. Occasionally, Myles did catch Tyrone gazing at her from far. His right eye was saying: *I want to call you 'Mom' and touch you, like any other kids in school. Why are we so far apart?* Yet he distanced himself from touching her. Tyrone did not resist touching Myles though, especially when he was in a playful mood. He would put his open palm at the base of Myles's nape and rub or pinch, like picking up a cat at its neck. Here, Myles was the one to tell him to stop it: his strength hurt Myles's neck. He would laugh and let Myles go.

At Josephine's house, Myles's room seemed twice as spacious as the old room he had shared with Tyrone in the Brooks Street house. The only furniture in Myles's room was his bed. He hung in the closet his trousers and two winter jackets and put on the shelf above the hanging bar his shirts, undershirts, underpants, and two crewneck sweaters—all neatly folded. This closet was large enough that Myles could bring in his bed and make it into a bedroom: a little cocoon. But then if he did it, his room would have turned into one big empty space, except for a brick-colored lamp with a tall, top-heavy vase-like shape sitting on the floor in one corner of the room. It was about this time that Myles became fond of having a lamp on the floor: he felt a certain closeness to this lamp emitting warm light quietly. He did not feel the same way with lamps on the side-tables in the house.

Tyrone came into Myles's room often, unannounced, and plunked himself down on Myles's bed. Since Myles had no furniture in the room, he always sat on his bed to do homework. Or to read one of the books he had pulled out of Josephine's one-bookcase home library. Tyrone sat near Myles, cross-legged.

"What are you doing?" Tyrone would ask, knowing exactly what Myles was doing.

Myles gathered Tyrone was still getting used to being alone in his own room. To get rid of him, Myles would say: "Let's go to the kitchen and get some sausage soup."

Tyrone never refused Myles's proposal: The leftover sausage soup that Josephine had cooked at the church was Tyrone's favorite. Tyrone would open the freezer, take out two frozen soups in hard plastic containers, put these icy masses into a pot, and turn on the gas flame low to melt the soup at a slow speed. When it had reached the boiling point, he would pour the steaming sausage soup into two bowls on the wooden kitchen table where Myles was sitting. Tyrone always served himself one of the two soups first, and then put the other soup in front of Myles. Sniffing the steamy taste of the soup seemed Tyrone's ritual. And then, with a large serving spoon the size wider than his mouth, Tyrone slurped his soup.

Myles chewed sausage and spinach, taking his time. The soup tasted the same most of the time. But then, from time to time, Josephine must have added extra sausage and garlic, which gave the soup a pungent meaty aroma. If Tyrone had ever noticed this delicious aroma, Myles had no idea. It seemed his only aim was to fill his mouth with all the ingredients that the soup contained. When he had finished his soup, without fail, Tyrone would stare at Myles's soup, saying nothing. Myles would put his half-filled bowl in front of Tyrone and take his empty bowl away. Those years Tyrone wanted, and needed, a lot of food. He was growing much faster than Myles was.

Light filled every room in their home—the boys' rooms on the second floor, Josephine's room on the first floor, and the living room. Even the narrow horizontal window above the sink let the bright afternoon sunlight across the cooking counter.

One day Tyrone came into Myles's room and went right to the window. The early afternoon sun illuminated his left-side profile. His left eye looked like a glass ball: it had no spark. His bridge had grown higher and sturdier, or so it appeared.

"What if we pulled out the Red Dragon maple from our old house and dragged it over here?" Tyrone said.

"I like that."

"Auntie's garden has got lots of flowers. But they all look like they're crawling on the ground."

"We need something higher?"

"Yeah, something tall. And plant it close to the house."

"Why you like that maple tree so much?"

"I don't know. It's not beautiful, like Auntie's flowers. The maple keeps growing all by itself. Nobody cares if it's there or not. The color of the leaves never changes—it's always dark red."

"Why don't you ask Auntie Jo? She can convince Grandmother Cora."

"I don't know."

"Ask her."

Tyrone looked at Myles as if to say: "Don't push me."

That night, after dinner, Josephine sat in her russet armchair, larger than her sister's chair at Brooks Street. Tyrone and Myles sat on the couch, Tyrone leaning forward and clasping his hands as he liked to do to indicate he was paying attention.

"The maple tree we talked about?" Josephine's gaze was on Tyrone. "I thought about it. I think we should keep the tree where it is." She sounded decisive. "Your grandmother cherishes it because your grandfather had planted it soon after they were married. I'm sure it means something to your mother, too."

"It's like nobody cares. It's just standing there," Tyrone said, preparing to argue his point.

"That's what makes it meaningful to them, don't you see?"

Myles said nothing.

"I have an idea, boys." Josephine's quick glance sought their responses. "Let's buy a new maple. It will be a tiny very young Bloodgood Japanese Maple. When it grows tall, it canopies. I want to get two more very small maples to plant either side of the Bloodgood—they will be Evergreen maples." She paused. "What do you think?"

"You have my vote, Auntie," Tyrone said.

"Me too."

"I'll water them. Give them some fertilizer, too."

"Me too."

Tyrone looked at Myles.

Josephine grinned.

Two days after the discussion, on a Saturday late morning, they all got in Josephine's Volkswagen and went to South Bend Nursery. They picked up a small Bloodgood and two small Evergreen maples with green leaves and slender trunks. Josephine suggested that they plant the maples below Myles's window; and that, since Tyrone favored maples, they switch their rooms so that Tyrone could look at the maples from his window any time he wanted. Myles went along with her at once. Tyrone's room, Myles had discovered, measured much smaller than his. When Josephine assigned these rooms to them, maybe she did not take the room size into consideration. Tyrone should have gotten Myles's room to begin with—he was much bigger than Myles was. From the window in Myles's new room, he had a skewed view of the maple trees. The sunlight gave them a sheen.

Every other late Saturday morning, Tyrone scattered powdered fertilizer between the young trees, drawing on the ground a double figure eight. He cared for the maple trees as if he would nurture birds in a cage. Myles often saw from his window Tyrone and Josephine weeding around the young maple trees. Myles knew Tyrone liked Josephine. So did Myles.

Josephine was different from her younger sister, nor was she much like her mother Cora. Josephine was a hugger—she loved people. Her hugs were long, strong, and warm.

Myles was unaware when he had come out of his cocoon, but he spoke to her with no fear. It took a while though to know that Josephine was delighted to hear him speak, and that she pushed their conversation forward, steering Myles to express himself naturally.

Josephine often put her arm across Tyrone's broad shoulders, but Myles had not seen him reciprocate her affection. It was no matter to her. She was more interested in his schoolwork, how he wanted to plan his future, if he wanted to stay in Mishawaka, or if he would be interested in attending University of Notre Dame in South Bend, which was sixteen miles from Mishawaka. Myles overheard Tyrone telling Josephine he disliked academic studies, except science like studies of living things such as insects, animals, plants. Even so he was not really into it—at least at that time, the year 1970.

Josephine had always taken Myles's stony silence for its face value.

"As you grow older, Myles, you will learn to crack your little cocoon," she told him. "You will be fun to talk to—I know."

Myles would throw his arms around her, gleeful that she did not see him as a pathetic child with inability to interact with children of his own age as well as with grownups.

"Until that time, read as many books as you can. You can borrow any book you want to read from the bookcase."

When she said this to him, Myles was taken aback: To him the word "book" had meant textbooks—and he detested them because they were part of school activity which he, too, hated because it often forced him to talk in class. But Josephine's library books impressed him in a different way. Housed in a floor-to-ceiling bookcase—not wide, but one narrow case with six shelves—the books, most of them in paperback, appeared waiting to be picked up. They exuded a sense of purpose. Myles stood in front of the bookcase and daydreamed what it would be to memorialize the contents of all these books into his brain. Would it be possible? The task seemed gigantic.

Josephine's kitchen looked nothing like the one at the Brooks Street house. She had three bright bulbs attached to the ceiling with a white plain casing protecting each bulb. A massive square freezer with two sliding glass sealers, placed next to the refrigerator, displayed stacks of food wrapped in waxed paper. Myles could not tell what they were because frost had covered them all. The motor attached to this large box kept on growling. Once Myles asked Tyrone what this box was. Tyrone said that Josephine volunteered at her church, cooking for the homeless, the sick, and the old. She delivered dinners to them, too. After her delivery, she brought home the leftovers of that day and put them in the ice box. She ate some leftovers. She took some of them to her neighbors. She never forgot to share the food with her fellow volunteers at church.

Before she became the boys' legal guardian and the boys moved in with her at her house four blocks away from the Brooks Street house, Josephine used to stop by Brooks Street twice a week for dinner. On each visit, she brought a potato sack full of frozen leftovers. On the days of Josephine's visits, Grandmother Cora took breaks. Josephine's visitations had a set schedule: She spent an hour with Grandmother Cora on the second floor, then took Cecilia outside for a walk, and had dinner with her and the boys in the porch.

One evening, Josephine grilled the leftover sandwiches she had brought with her, boiled pasta and meatballs, and heated soups. By the time they finished their dinner, the desserts left out on the kitchen table had defrosted just so. Cecilia and Josephine had coffee with their desserts, Tyrone had a large glass of iced tea, and Myles a cup of milk. Myles liked the way she cooked her leftovers—the food tasted as if they were cooked just now, fresh. Josephine washed the dirty dishes, and

Tyrone volunteered to dry them. Tyrone used a rag the size of a bath towel. Maybe it used to be a bath towel. Myles was left with Cecilia in the porch.

Cecilia sat in a wicker armchair by the window. Myles pulled his hard chair by her.

"You are getting taller every day, son, aren't you?" Cecilia said.

"Tyrone's bigger, Mom."

"Well, he is your big brother, hon. So, he is much bigger than you are."

Myles smiled while thinking: *A younger brother can be a giant and his older brother can look like a dwarf.*

Cecilia's blank gaze stayed beyond the treetops in the wood on the far end of their backyard.

They both fell silent.

Cecilia showed no sign that she was aware Myles was looking at the side view of her face. Unlike Grandmother Cora, Cecilia had a small egg-shaped face. Her eyelids covered her eyeballs halfway over: they opened, then half-closed, slowly—Myles expected her to start nodding. But he guessed this was how her eyelids moved. The right corner of her mouth twitched as if she was sucking on something like a jellybean, or cleaning with her tongue the spaces between teeth to get rid of food particles stuck there. Her lips wrinkled and stretched in turn and pushed up her nose a little.

"A delicious dinner it was," Cecilia muttered to herself. "The dessert, too."

Myles wanted to say to her so badly: *Oh, that was so sweet—a cake with cream in between and ice cream on top!* But his right hand had quickly covered his mouth, not to say anything because she might ask him what kind of dessert it was. He could not have answered her—he did not know the name of the cake. And if he had tried to answer her, he would have gone into a panic and his heart would race in fear of being laughed at. Cecilia never laughed at Myles, though. But he had been laughed at countless times at school. And every time he felt he had to talk, warmth in every part of his body froze with fear. Which forced him to jump right back into his cocoon.

Cecilia's vacant gaze floated above Brooks Street that peeked out between their neighbors' houses. A boy Myles's age flashed through the street on his bike.

A long silence partitioned Cecilia from Myles at the window. Drowning must feel like this—pushed underwater against his will, sinking, never hit the bottom.

Cecilia's head tilted, and her eyes closed. Myles wanted to say to her "Mom, are you well?" He touched her arm gently, instead. She jerked as if by electric shock and abruptly moved away from Myles in the wicker armchair. The size of her eyes, and their darkness, startled Myles. They stared at each other. Cecilia then shifted her focus on to Brooks Street.

I don't belong here, Myles thought. He stood up and put his chair back to the table. The sound of water shooting from the faucet in the kitchen continued. Every time Josephine had come over and had dinner and washed dishes, she let out powerful hot water. That evening was no exception. Tyrone was still wiping dishes: His dishrag must be getting wet and smelly. Myles retreated to the room which he had shared with Tyrone ever since he was a toddler.

His hands tucked under his thighs, Myles sat on his bed asking himself if he should ever go into the porch with his mother again. Cecilia's abrupt move in the armchair had signaled to him that, when she was in the porch, she wanted to be alone. She must have tolerated the brothers. Myles wondered if Tyrone felt the same way, or if Tyrone knew something about Cecilia that Myles did not. And if Tyrone did, how could he have learned it? From someone he knew? A thirteen-year-old would know more than an eleven-year-old would: the two-year difference in age—Tyrone had to have come across more people than Myles had. Myles had thought of asking him about Cecilia. On second thought, he decided not to: he wanted to avoid another uppercut in the jaw.

The door squeaked open, and Tyrone peeked in. "You want to go to Auntie Jo's?" He awaited Myles's response. "We can have more leftovers."

"Is mother going with us?"

"She wants to stay home."

Myles went to the window and looked down at the curbside in front of the house.

"C'mon, boys," Josephine yelled, already standing outside her light gray Volkswagen with four doors. She had driven this boxy car ever since Myles could remember.

When Myles stepped outside, he was stunned—Tyrone was sitting in the driver's seat and Josephine in the passenger seat.

"You sit in the back, brother."

"Don't worry, Myles. Your big brother already knows how to drive. I'm going to let him drive from here to my house. Just four blocks— maybe he can go around the block three times."

"What if—"

"I bump into a telephone pole?" Tyrone stared at Myles, confident. "We all die."

Myles rolled into the back seat behind Josephine. The car backed up and then moved forward. He looked at the driver's seat to make sure Tyrone was driving—without his left eye. Josephine seemed unaffected by his impairment. But Tyrone would not be able to get his license for a few more years until he had turned sixteen. Myles had five more years to wait for this privilege.

Tyrone headed right into Josephine's garage. This was the first time Myles ever witnessed a half-blind guy driving, following traffic signs and maintaining a level speed. As Myles recalled, it had taken him five more years to know that a human body could function with one of a pair: the eye, the kidney, the lung.

"Good job." Josephine patted Tyrone. She then got out of the car. And, going around the hood of the car, she turned the garage light on and opened the door that led into the kitchen. Myles followed her. Tyrone followed Myles.

"May I have a hot coffee, Auntie Jo?" Tyrone asked.

"Why not?" Josephine said. "And Myles can have a glass of iced tea. How's that sound?"

Myles nodded to them both. "With sugar, please."

She brought in three drinks on a wooden tray and put the tray on the coffee table. "Okay, boys. Help yourselves."

Myles sat on the floor, cross-legged. She had put a lot of sugar in his iced tea, in a tall glass—some of the sugar stuck over the ice cubes, some had gone down to the bottom and accumulated. The aroma of coffee cleared his nasal passage. He wanted to taste Tyrone's coffee.

"So ... I was talking to Father Evans at my church the other day," she said just as soon as she sunk into her ultra-soft couch.

"What about?" Tyrone leaned forward, his elbows on his knees. "Us?"

"Who else would I talk about? You two are my precious stones. You know, your uncle has been gone a long time now. My mother is too busy taking care of my sister."

"Do we have cousins anywhere?"

Josephine stopped still. She then sipped her coffee, sidestepping Tyrone's question. "Father Evans doesn't think much of Blessed Mary School. But, don't you know, it's been around for a long time. I went there. Your mother did too, but she dropped out when she finished sixth grade."

"Where else can we go if not Blessed Mary?"

"That's what we were talking about. Father Evans knows a good boarding school for boys. It's far away."

Tyrone's face lit up. "How far is 'far away'?"

"Philadelphia." She got up, went to the bookcase, and pulled out an atlas from the lowest shelf. "Come over here, Tyrone." She opened the page that focused on the eastern half of the United States. And, tracing the highways on the map with her index finger, she showed the distance between Mishawaka, Indiana and Philadelphia, Pennsylvania.

Tyrone sighed. "That is far."

"Greyhound will take you there."

"If I go there, who's going to pay the tuition, lodging, and food?"

"All included in the scholarship if you get it. You have to apply for it."

Tyrone suddenly turned pensive.

Myles surmised that Josephine had already spoken to Father Evans about our schooling, and that Father Evans had a connection with the boarding school in Philadelphia. Tyrone could transfer there if he could pass the examination. Could life be this smooth? Would they accept Tyrone, with a problem with managing his anger—the kind of anger that could erupt when least expected?

"Scholarship?" Tyrone said. "I won't get it."

"You're good with science," Josephine said.

"Yeah, but …"

Tyrone must want to get away from his mother, grandmother, this tiny country town of Mishawaka and memories that lived with it all, and from his younger brother included, too, who could hardly articulate his thoughts—Myles surmised. What if Josephine had asked Myles if he wanted to go to Philadelphia? Would he go? Myles did not know. Philadelphia sounded like the eastern end of the world. A boarding school meant he would have to live with other boys from all over the country—just thinking about these things, Myles got horrified. What would he do if he were bullied? Tyrone would not be there to protect him, like here at Blessed Mary. The only good thing would be the boys would be on scholarship.

"Father Evans already looked at your transcripts, Tyrone."

"How could he? He is just a priest."

"The church is Catholic, so is Blessed Mary. He has an inside connection." Josephine's still gaze stayed on Tyrone's profile which was half hidden in his hands. "You don't need to decide right away, dear. Think about it."

That night, when they had gone back to Brooks Street, Tyrone stayed in the living room until eleven o'clock. Myles was in his room, unable to fall asleep, just looking up at the ceiling. Myles sneaked out of the room and stood at the door, watching Tyrone sitting alone in the flattened old couch.

"Come here, Myles."

Myles sat by Tyrone, but distancing himself from his brother.

"Closer."

Tyrone put his left arm around Myles's shoulder.

Myles stayed still. He could not sever the thought that Josephine might be planning to send both boys away to Philadelphia, into somebody else's hands, which would free herself from all this.

Myles wanted Tyrone to stay in Mishawaka.

Poker

Memorial Hospital phoned Myles, begging him over to the hospital at once. It was one o'clock in the morning.

"Right away—" Myles said and put down the receiver. The other party had said nothing about Tyrone's condition suddenly turning for the worse. Myles was relieved. Still, he felt jolted in fear that Tyrone might have caused an accident, and that Myles himself could be held responsible for Tyrone damaging hospital properties.

Myles put his jeans on, his khaki short-sleeved shirt untucked. He then dashed out of his apartment, hopped into his black Mercury, and turned on the ignition. Approaching the hospital, he saw his headlights were off. He quickly turned them on and looked all around the car. Dimly lit buildings passed by—dark gray. He was the only one on the highway driving toward the hospital.

When Myles hurried off the elevator, the nurse supervisor for the night shift stuck her head from Room 220 and waved at him to hurry up.

Myles marched into the room. The nurse-supervisor grabbed his arm and said, "Not so fast."

"You bastard, you! Why the hell did you put me in this damn nursing home here!" Tyrone's rage shook the room. "I'm going home!"

How could he have this much energy?, Myles wondered as he stood bolt upright. The image of Tyrone's flaccid body draped over the wheelchair returned, smacking Myles's brain: *No, not another stroke!*

"Tyrone." With suppressed gentleness, Myles held Tyrone's arms. "I'm Myles, your brother. Don't you see?" Myles realized Tyrone's oxygen tube was gone, his IV tube dangling from the plastic bag that still contained the liquid halfway, and the back of his right-hand bleeding, with the transparent bandage peeled off. He froze at the J-tube laying near his pillow. Blood had stained the tip of the J-tube. "Tyrone! You didn't!" Myles pulled up Tyrone's hospital garment: the J-tube hole agape, and a string of blood dividing his abdomen in two. "Lie down." Myles touched Tyrone's shoulder and attempted to raise his legs up on the bed.

"Get away from me, you traitor! No wonder your mother didn't want you!" Tyrone pushed Myles away and, grabbing the metal bar at the foot of the bed, tottered to the closet where Myles had stacked up a few clean undershirts and briefs the day before. Tyrone's breath suddenly turned rough, and he nearly fell on the floor.

As if by reflex the nurse's hands shielded her mouth, her eyes goggling in fear.

Myles caught him by his back and, holding his left forearm, led him back to his bed.

"This is Memorial Hospital. Not a nursing home, brother." Myles picked up the bloody J-tube staining the bottom sheet and handed it to the nurse. Then he lay Tyrone down on his bed—his head on the pillow first, and then his legs up. He put the oxygen tube nimbly back into Tyrone's nostril.

Stunned by the realization that he could not move fast enough to get his clothes, Tyrone kept following Myles's movement with his right eye.

"Could you give him some sedative?" Myles asked.

"Let me call Dr. Canon, to make sure."

"Could you tell her about the J-tube, too?"

"Certainly." The nurse-supervisor left the room.

Myles turned to Tyrone and sat at the edge of his bed. "Can you breathe all right?"

Tyrone nodded once and gazed into Myles's eyes, then to his own toes. He was silent.

Myles was uncertain what this silence meant. There was no clue.

Tyrone clasped Myles's hand in his. "I'm glad you're here," Tyrone whispered.

"Quiet, brother. Quiet." Myles kept Tyrone's hand in his.

The nurse-supervisor returned with a young doctor in a light blue uniform. He pulled out a pair of purple surgical gloves and put them on with an agile hand movement. The nurse handed a filled syringe to him.

"Just a small amount of Lorazepam," the doctor said while focusing on the liquid going inside Tyrone's upper arm. "This should make you feel better." He then exchanged the syringe with a new J-tube in a sealed plastic bag that the nurse was holding behind him. "It'll be a minute or so." The doctor unsealed the J-tube and removed Tyrone's garment from the left end to expose the J-tube hole. The nurse disinfected the wound. The doctor bent over to get a good view of Tyrone's abdomen. He then slowly inserted the tube into his intestine. The nurse was standing by him with three layers of split drain sponge gauze. The doctor peeled two layers from the nurse's hand and put them around Tyrone's tube to secure it.

"All done," the doctor said as if to himself, removing his purple gloves.

Tyrone's eyes were half open. Soon he would be asleep.

Tyrone had asked the nurse to keep the curtain on the window side open until the dawn. That night, Myles stayed with Tyrone in Room 220, sleeping on the cushioned bench by the window.

A night light by the door emitted an anemic glow. Lying on the cushion, with his hands under his head, Myles stayed wide awake. What made Tyrone think he was in a nursing home? Myles kept asking himself. Tyrone screaming "traitor" echoed in every part of his brain. And what was Myles's mother not wanting him? Hadn't Dr. Canon been giving him a Prozac-Zyprexa combo since the day he was admitted? When Myles released Tyrone's medical data to the administrator he spoke with, Myles was certain he mentioned that Tyrone had bipolar disorder, and that he was on Prozac for its treatment. Since Myles moved in with Tyrone in the early fall of 2011, Tyrone had shown no major indications of manic depression, rage, verbal abuse. Myles was starting to trust this Prozac therapy. Maybe Lorazepam would be more effective. If so, Myles would not complain; he would go along with Dr. Canon—he determined.

Myles turned to Tyrone's quiet profile. Where did that energy come from, despite the stroke and almost dying? Tyrone had been driven by unpredictability since he was a boy. And this unpredictability frightened Myles. What if Tyrone did something stupid and hurt himself. Or somebody else?

⁂

The day following Thanksgiving Day in 1970, Tyrone and Myles raked snow away from the short path in front of their Brooks Street house. The snow had fallen the night before—much earlier than previous years as

Myles remembered. After shoveling away the crusted snow, Tyrone and Myles brought out the potbelly stove from their basement. Tyrone was muscular for his age, but he was not strong enough to pull it out alone: he needed Myles's help. While they were dragging the iron stove and parts of the tin funnel out of the storage closet, Grandmother Cora, with her hands on her stout hips, stood at the base of the staircase. She was watching the boys as if Myles, not Tyrone, might steal something she had kept in a faded brown cedar bureau there in the basement and cherished whatever it was in it for years, though most likely without ever opening the bureau. Myles knew this because every time he came down to the basement, there she scrutinized him. She seemed to sense when Myles was heading down there. Maybe the air that filled the house trembled after him, and her skin picked it up. She followed him on her toes. Sometimes she would mumble: "Don't you get close to my bureau, Little One." Myles hated it when she called him "Little One." It was her way of making him feel smaller and more powerless than he was. Her warning stirred his curiosity, though. Myles stared at this old chest wondering what was in it that valued so much she had to come down to the basement to protect it from his possible theft. He had no intention of stealing anything—he just wanted to look at it. He guessed the treasure could be a bracelet his great-grandmother had bought at Woolworth, or her wedding ring she could no longer wear because her finger had grown fat and dry with old age.

The potbelly stove must have been one of the residents of this house for years. The middle part of the stove's belly had rusted and turned brick color. Until that year nobody had taken care of the stove, Myles suspected. Tyrone, with an ash tool poker, scrubbed its belly from the left side of the opening, to get rid of the rust. The metallic screech penetrated Myles's brain. To help hasten the removal of the rust, Myles scrubbed the stove from the right side of the opening with a paint scraper that he had found on the shelf above where the stove had been. Tyrone stopped. He came around to where Myles was on his knees, scouring.

"Not bad."

"So?" Myles turned to the staircase. Grandmother Cora was not there. He went around to see Tyrone's scrub job. "Your side is scratchy."

"I guess iron against iron." Tyrone returned to his side, making the screechy noise once again.

Myles stared at how Tyrone's big hand manipulated the poker. His hand motion was minimal, but it could give a hard pressure against the belly. Myles went back to his side.

"Did you hear, Myles?" Tyron's hand continued to move with precision.

"What?"

"Clem McCullum."

"I saw a man the other day. With Mother, in the porch."

"That's him. Large, and stinks like a bull."

"Isn't he our dad?" Myles meant it seriously.

"Are you kidding?" Tyrone stopped scrubbing. "I don't know who our fathers are—"

"We have different fathers?" Myles nearly choked at this surprise.

"I don't know, brother. I haven't asked Auntie Jo."

"Is she supposed to know about our father, or maybe fathers?"

"If there's anybody in our family who knew about our father, it's Auntie Jo."

"How come?"

"She got antennas all over her head."

Although it bothered Myles that Tyrone and he might have two different men as their fathers, they never talked about it. Then Clem McCullum appeared on the scene; and Tyrone was suddenly talking about their father or fathers. Is Clem our father? Myles refused to believe Clem could be his father. Tyrone liked only a handful of people—Clem was not one of them. This, Myles knew for sure.

"But his last name is McCullum," Tyrone said. "Ours is Odam—you, me, and mother."

"What's Auntie Jo's last name?"

"Isn't it Floden? If I remember it right."

"She was always Auntie Jo to me."

"She was married to a Norwegian—our uncle. That's all I know."

"Why is Clem here, then?"

"I don't know."

"Is he mother's new husband?"

"Maybe a new boyfriend … Just to play with."

"Mother? Just to play with?" Myles could not picture what she would do with Clem.

"A friend. A good friend. To do things with … You know."

"How do you mean?"

Tyrone smiled.

He had no reason to smile at me like that—at that moment, Myles resented Tyrone.

"You are talking, little brother."

Myles realized he was outside his cocoon. But then, with Tyrone, Myles had often found himself outside his cocoon. Tyrone always made Myles forget he had the fear of speaking to people. If Tyrone and Myles had different fathers, Myles hardly gave a thought to it. They were born of the same mother, and this made them brothers. Myles was okay with that.

They set the potbelly stove by the door that opened to the porch. This was the place in the living room where mother and Grandmother Cora had placed the stove before. This year Grandmother Cora asked Tyrone and Myles to do the job since they were big and strong enough in her opinion. It was cumbersome to put the funnel parts together: stacking the two long tin cylindrical pieces one on the other toward the ceiling, and then fitting a horizontal piece linking the top of the cylindrical piece to a hole from which another long horizontal piece extended right under the porch ceiling that pushed out through a hole on the wall out on to a short vertical chimney with a conical roof attached to it.

Until the previous year, Grandmother Cora had lit the stove. This year Tyrone lit a fire on a crumbled newspaper inside the stove. The flame spread on to the two pieces of bone-dry firewood he had thrown in. Myles squatted behind Tyrone and watched the flame flare up. Soon the flame was growling, and then the heat generated in the living room. Myles crawled backward on his butt, his face turning red. Tyrone backed from the potbelly stove and sat on the floor cross-legged, watching the flame, satisfied that he could do a better job than his grandmother. He wrapped a thick layer of rug around his right hand and closed the stove's iron door. And he positioned a set of fireplace-tools by the stove: the iron spatula, the course brush, and the poker that looked like the beak of a kite—all with thirty-inch handles.

A week before Christmas, Clem McCullum suddenly became a new member of their household. He shared Cecilia's room with her, as there was no other room available in our house. Cecilia had not told her sons who this large man with red face and golden beard was. Maybe it did not matter to her whether the boys got to know him or not. He called their grandmother "Gran'mama." He ignored the boys. Whenever he passed across the living room, a weird odor lingered on behind him. Tyrone and Myles decided that he was so large, and his arms were so short, that he could not keep his rear end clean. They were happy to see Clem did not join them in the porch for dinner. He and Grandmother Cora had their dinner together in the kitchen. The boys never knew what they talked about over their food—they did not care. Sometimes Cecilia joined Clem and grandmother in the kitchen. It was all right with the boys: Cecilia hardly spoke to the boys at dinner table in the porch, anyway.

One night, Tyrone was startled by a sound.

"Do you hear that?" he asked.

"What?" Myles didn't hear anything unusual.

"Somebody is crying."

"It's so late at night."

"Shh!" Tyrone said. "Listen."

Myles sat up on his bed. So did Tyrone. Now Myles heard it—the crying Tyrone had heard a few seconds ago. It was more like sobbing. Quivering whispers interrupted the sobbing at times. The louder the whispers, the more intense the squeaking of the old bed. Tyrone's eyes focused on a spot on the worn-out rug that covered the floor. Myles drew back against his headboard and hugged his pillow. He could see Tyrone's right eye shooting a red beam of alert as if a panther getting ready to attack. "Tyrone!"

Tyrone did not hear Myles's hoarse voice. He hurried to the door, grabbed the door handle with both hands, and turned it without a sound. He stood there, and, tiptoeing, he inched toward the potbelly stove that was still nursing the leftovers of burnt firewood.

Myles followed Tyrone to the doorway of their bedroom, anticipating nothing.

Tyrone picked up a rag and covered the handle of the iron poker that he had laid by the stove before they went to bed. Squatting, Tyrone butchered the burnt firewood into pieces with the poker. Sparks flared up in all directions. Flames reignited. He threw in a small firewood to get more heat and stirred once more. He left the tip of the poker in the flame. He remained squatting, staring into the flame as if hypnotized by its orange power that could extinguish anything. The flame reflected across Tyrone's face, turning his face gold.

Myles moved toward Tyrone, to squat with him, to ask if he was all right. He showed no sign of awareness Myles was coming near him.

"Don't!" Tyrone said.

Myles stepped back.

Tyrone grabbed the poker-handle and stood up. The flame had reddened half of the thirty-inch iron bar including its hooked tip.

Sobbing and whispers, meshed into the rhythmical squeaks of the bed, turned louder.

Tyrone, with the burning iron poker, dashed to the room next to the front foyer of the house, and kicked the door open.

The burning poker sliced the air.

The poker pierced Clem's bare butt and gouged out a piece of tissue from him.

With his roar, Clem's entire naked body sprang up and landed on the other side of Cecilia.

Tyrone raised the poker once again.

Clem fell on the floor, thrashing about in a pang of the deep burn agape and bloody.

"Tyrone! He's your father!" Cecilia screamed, abruptly hiding her breasts with the top sheet. "Get out of here, you devil!"

Tyrone drew backward, still holding the poker, his face beat red.

Outside Cecilia's room, Grandmother Cora was talking on the phone.

The emergency siren shattered the night, turning louder toward Brooks Street.

Secrets

"No. Prozac wasn't in my med-cocktail—I don't think." Tyrone hesitated.

"What do you mean, 'I don't think'?"

"I didn't see my nurse breaking a blue capsule into the mix."

Myles got up from the visitor's chair and stepped over to the foot board of Tyrone's bed where his medical chart hung. He picked up the chart and went down the list, with his index finger tracing each item.

"No Prozac," he said. "Oh, here it is—Lorazepam. They switched your depression pill, Tyrone."

"They did?"

"Yeah. Here, look."

Tyrone scanned the chart and nodded his agreement.

Myles hung the chart back on the hook on the foot board. "You want your head up a little more?"

"No. I'm good. Go down to the cafeteria and get something to eat."

"In a minute."

"You haven't eaten much since I yelled at you." Tyrone's right eye sparkled for a second. "I'm sorry, Myles. I've been a pain in the butt since I was born."

"We are okay, Tyrone." Myles was dying to ask Tyrone what he had meant when he said, amid his violent rage two days ago, that their mother didn't want Myles. Did Tyrone mean that mother wanted to give Myles away for adoption? Did he mean just to throw him in an orphanage? Did he mean she wanted to abort Myles when she was pregnant with him? Myles could only wait for the right moment for these questions—he did not want to cause Tyrone another round of stroke or heart attack. Tyrone would have to start talking about it: this would be the sign that they could discuss it. But "when" was the big question. Tyrone might never initiate this conversation again, or he might flow into the discussion out of blue sky—tomorrow, today, maybe when Myles had come back from the cafeteria early that afternoon.

"You okay, now?" Myles asked and tucked Tyrone's top sheet under his chin.

Tyrone chuckled. "Brother, you can be a mother."

"Just for now." As Myles headed for the cafeteria in the basement, a nurse entered the room.

"Good morning," the nurse said. "I'm Joyce. I'll be taking care of you until four o'clock today. If you need anything, just press the buzzer." She put down on the adjustable bedside table two cans with the same labels: Jevity 1.5 Cal. And from the cupboard she took out a sealed syringe with no needle attached to it. She poured a can and half of Jevity into a cylindrical plastic container without a lid. "Your breakfast, Mr. Odam." With one hand she drew the liquid into the syringe, and with the thumb of the other hand she flipped the small round lid of the J-tube open.

Tyrone kept gazing at the cream-colored liquid food going down into his body through the tube. When the tube was empty, the nurse injected more liquid into the tube.

"Does that feel okay?" the nurse asked.

"In a way," Tyrone said. "I don't get hungry. But then I never get a full stomach."

"You lost weight a little, Mr. Odam, since you were admitted here. We have to fatten you up."

"This creamy stuff will do the job, you think?"

"We'll see." Joyce gave Tyrone an instantaneous smile which at once disappeared from her smooth-skinned face. "By the way, Mr. Odam, you are scheduled to return to rehab on Monday—it'll be your fourth and final week here."

"Yes, ma'am." Tyrone thought this was an appropriate response to the tone of her voice, and her quick smile.

The nurse packed up her medical gadgets on the tray she had brought in and left the room.

Tyrone had no idea what the hospital cafeteria would serve staff and visitors. He was certain that Myles would have at least two cups of coffee with plenty of sugar there at the cafeteria, and probably would bring up an additional cup of coffee when he would come back to Tyrone's room. Tyrone stretched sideways to get his water and the sponge on the table. Ice cubes filled the pliable plastic cup, some of which had melted into water. He sucked water out of the green sponge head, and then licked—curious of the sandpaper-like sensation the sponge was giving his tongue.

Myles returned. "What are you laughing about?"

"I just knew you'd come back with a coffee."

"I can't help it. I'm addicted to it."

"The smell hits you, doesn't it?"

"You remember when Auntie Jo gave you a cup of coffee for the first time? Man, did that smell great."

"I loved Josephine. How long has it been since she passed on?"

"I was forty-seven—so it's been six years."

"She knew a lot."

"No doubt."

"You know, she moved to Denver after she married our Uncle Marvin."

"I remember Auntie Jo said she married when she was seventeen. She was an outsider most of her life, then."

"Yeah, Josephine didn't think like grandmother or our mother—I guess they didn't think much of anything, anyway."

"Did Auntie Jo ever tell you about our father—or fathers?"

"Strange you ask that now."

"I always wondered about that—our mother being such a social butterfly in her younger days."

"You remember when I stabbed Clem's butt with an iron poker? I was thirteen and thought mother was in real danger. Mother yelled at me Clem was my father—I bet her head was all screwed up, then."

"I asked Auntie Jo about that once. She didn't answer me straight."

"Maybe she couldn't."

"Why you think that?"

"You know that our mother was a well-known prostitute around South Bend, right? She must've slept with tons of guys. Two seeds happened to hit her ovary at two different times, and we were born, Myles."

"People always said we looked like twins."

"Maybe we took after our mother."

"Auntie Jo mentioned a man named Benjamin Odam, Tyrone. He was living with mother and grandmother in the Brooks Street house for some time. But then Auntie was in Denver, so she couldn't be sure of anything back in Mishawaka in those days."

"Yeah—" Tyrone looked at the window. "We carry his last name. But it doesn't mean he fathered us, or you, or me. I don't know."

"Someone told me I could be Emma's son. Did you know who that was?"

"Oh, good God! Josephine's older sister Emma? She was a slut. Our mother and Emma were known as 'The Petticoat Sisters'."

"'The Petticoat Sisters?!' Is that an insult?" Myles burst out laughing.

Tyrone followed Myles, his mild laugh turning into a cough. He at once sucked the cold sponge, and the cough subsided.

"Are you okay? I didn't mean to make you laugh. I just couldn't help it. The Petticoat Sisters—" Myles suppressed his laugh, his abdomen shaking.

Tyrone, with his tongue, kept squeezing water from the sponge. Knowing Myles was getting a kick out of his story brought a spark in Tyrone's right eye.

"Where did you hear that?"

"Josephine. Who else? I know she heard it from some of her church people—you know, they gossip like anybody else."

"I didn't know Auntie Jo had an older sister."

"Emma and our mother were close, Josephine said. Sometimes they worked together."

"Worked together? How?"

"You know, like sex work. Like sharing connections, and all." Tyrone nodded to no one in particular. "Josephine thought they had some underground connections with people like the mayor of Mishawaka, politicians in South Bend and even Chicago. But she made it clear that it came from people she knew. So, it was all rumor—no evidence."

"You knew all this, but you never told me about any of it, Tyrone. For years."

"How could I. We lived so far apart—you in Mishawaka, me in Cherry Hill."

"And that was since you graduated from Mount Olive High School in Philly."

"Four decades ago," Tyrone said, muttering to himself. "Grandmother Cora died, mother passed away, and Josephine's gone now—too."

"What happened to Emma?"

"She was twenty years old when she died. You know—syphilis. She died in the Brooks Street house. Her birthplace."

Air escaped Myles's chest. He regretted asking about Emma. He did not have to know about her. She had lived years and years ago. Why now? Why was Myles so concerned about an aunt he did not know until now over his coffee.

Silence stood between the siblings.

Myles took two more sips of coffee and sighed.

Tyrone dipped the green sponge in the ice-water and sucked it, in a leisurely pace. He was aware he had been talking too much—he was getting thirsty faster than usual. "Are you coming back tomorrow? It's Sunday."

"Sure. You know, I don't go to church."

Tyrone smiled and shook his head, casting a skewed gaze at Myles. "That's what our mother did after Emma died."

"Go to church? I mean, she returned to her faith?"

"Not for long. She started deteriorating—mentally. Like forgetting how to get to the church, sitting by the porch window for hours at a time."

"I hardly have any memory of touching mother, hugging her. She was far away." Myles sensed his arteries on both sides of his neck pulsate. He did not want to cause any trouble for Tyrone, but he had a question he felt he must ask.

Casting a pensive gaze of his right eye between his bed and the cushion below the window, Tyrone seemed prepared to take a weighty issue, a consequential question Myles was about to hurl at him.

"Tyrone," Myles said in a soft singing voice. "You and me—are we both mental cases?"

"You mean, you with severe anxiety disorder and me with bipolar disorder?"

"And the rest of the family weird?"

"Yes, Myles—we are."

"Do you think it runs in the family?"

"Maybe. I don't really know." Tyrone picked up an ice cube from the plastic cup, then put it in his mouth, and held it there: testing its glacial sensation. "My issue is why I was born with poor sight in my left eye. I do remember seeing blurred images through my left eye but they got darker and darker. And when I was six, the eye no longer took in any images. It has never seen a ray of light since. Why?"

Myles leaned forward and held Tyrone's arm. "You don't mean—"

Tyrone nodded with certainty, his right eye gripping his younger brother's expanded light-brown eyes.

"Syphilis," Tyrone said, dropping the horrific word.

"You and me?"

Tyrone gave Myles the same confident nod.

"No, Tyrone! No!" Myles yelled. His voice quickly turned into an accentuated intensity. "That's why mother stayed so far away from us."

Tyrone and Myles clutched each other's arms. Myles's hand, then, lost its grip and dropped onto his knee.

Basilica

JOYCE, THE NURSE, stopped Myles when he got off the elevator and was about to turn right toward Room 220.

"You'll need to put on some protective garments, gloves, and a headcover."

"Why—may I ask?" Myles resisted Joyce's urgent command. "I've never had to."

"You do now, Myles." Joyce leaned on the visitor services counter toward Myles. "Dr. Canon is in until three o'clock this afternoon. Let me see if she can see and speak to you about your brother's developing condition."

"A developing condition? What's developing?"

"I am referring you to Dr. Canon. She will answer all of your questions." Nurse Joyce came around the counter. "Could you please follow me?"

What makes you feel so superior to me—you're nothing but a nurse just out of college, Myles thought. Following her Myles stared at her straight back that indented slightly above her tail bone from which protruded a large pear-shaped butt. He pictured himself touching her plump behind.

Joyce turned around. "Dr. Canon's office." She smiled and showed him the door that was half cracked open.

"Myles Odam is here, Doctor," Joyce said, standing outside the door.

"Send him in."

Joyce opened the door all the way for Myles.

Dr. Canon stood up to greet Myles, and then urged him to sit down in an unadorned straight chair. She plunged right in: "Tyrone must stay here a few more weeks."

"What's wrong with him, Doctor?"

"He has something called C. diff, a simple abbreviation for the bacteria *Clostridioides difficile*. Patients on antibiotic therapy tend to get infected by it. And I'm afraid your brother has it. It was confirmed yesterday. He had an accident while you were gone. The color and texture of his stools looked suspicious, so we ran some testing."

Myles understood her matter-of-fact way of information delivery and found her open and natural tone of voice pleasing.

"How long does he have to stay here?"

"Until he tests absolutely clear of C. diff indications. C. diff is highly infectious. You must be extremely careful. Wear the hospital-provided protective gear while with him and wash your hands constantly."

"How is Tyrone—overall?"

"He's been losing weight—which is not a good sign. His heart shows some signs of anomaly."

"Meaning?"

"Arrythmia, for example—uneven pulses."

Myles, with his gaze fixed on Dr. Canon's translucent grayish-blue eyes, nodded his understanding of her information sharing.

"Now I need to make certain Tyrone's data we have are correct."

"Yes, Doctor."

"Tyrone has appointed you the executor of his will, and you have his power of attorney as well."

"That is all correct."

"And the living will?"

"He has it. I submitted a copy of it on the second day Tyrone was admitted here at Memorial."

"Are you also his health care representative?"

"Yes."

"Tyrone had a major stroke. He now has developed C. diff. His heart and lungs are weak. All those medical facts lead me to suggest to you, Myles, that you speak to him about his finances." Dr. Canon paused before speaking again. "The human body is an amazing machine. But it comes with unpredictability. It is wise to prepare for any probability."

"Are you saying—"

"No. All I'm saying is that preparation leads us to smooth transactions." With a black straight pen, she tapped her desk. "Now you must excuse me: I have a meeting to get to." She rose from her maroon leather chair.

Myles stood up.

Dr. Canon ushered him to the door.

"I'm here if you need me, Myles."

"Thank you, Doctor." Myles's hoarse voice stayed in his mouth.

Dr. Canon locked her office and headed for the opposite end of the hallway.

Myles meant to get off the elevator on the second floor. But he decided to go up to the sixth floor: he had seen a small room with a double entrance door above which was a sign, "Meditation Room." It took a few minutes, but he did find the room.

He opened the door on the right side. It gave out no noise. Myles entered the room. There were four pews on either side of the aisle, each pew measuring about six feet. This hexagonal room had a narrow window cut out about twenty inches from the ceiling. Walnut-brown varnish coated each of the six wall panels, showing their natural grains. It rang a bell for Myles—he had seen something like these walls before, something serene and confusing.

⁂

It was 1974 when Myles, then a fifteen-year-old boy, tagged along with Tyrone to the University of Notre Dame in South Bend. Tyrone had an appointment to see an admissions officer there at the University for a preliminary visit. Myles rode a Greyhound bus with Tyrone from Mishawaka to South Bend. The wind swirled in as the bus drove forward, bringing in the aroma of pasture tinged with cattle manure. Myles had known this summery aroma since he was still a toddler running around in a pair of shorts. The black pair of dress pants Tyrone was wearing that day made his legs longer than usual. He kept tightening and loosening his blue-and-maroon striped tie. Myles was in polo shirt and shorts, both of which had been his favorites—but lately the pants had gotten a bit tight around the waist. Tyrone sat near the driver, on the right side of the aisle. Myles went to sit all the way back on the left side where the seat could bounce harder than those in the front. Myles loved the bouncing. Sometimes he wished the seat would throw him up harder so that his head would hit the ceiling. A sense of staying in the air for a few seconds was what he was after, though it was hardly possible at his age and size.

Every now and then Myles would look at Tyrone. Tyrone had not moved since the bus left Mishawaka. Tyrone had kept his chin rested on his hand, looking at the expanse of pasture, corn fields, aged farmhouses with horses tethered to palings. Tyrone had said often how he hated studying. If he had stayed away from studying, how could he pass examinations? Myles too hated studying, but Myles had to do his homework every night; otherwise, he would flunk courses. Maybe Tyrone could get by without studying and receive good grades—some people were born that way.

"Notre Dame," the driver said.

Tyrone turned around and gestured for Myles to come to the front. Tyrone stood up and, looking down at his feet, stepped down onto the pavement. Myles followed him. They headed straight to the main building with the golden dome. Inside, Myles waited while Tyrone spoke to a receptionist sitting behind a desk empty except for only a telephone.

"I have to go to the second floor," Tyrone said.

"Okay. I'll just look around a bit."

"Be back here in an hour. Say, by one-thirty?"

Myles nodded.

Tyrone did not use the elevator. He opted for the stairs.

Myles stepped outside.

The Basilica of the Sacred Heart stood west of the main hall. Artsy stuff, like paintings, sculptures, historical buildings, and the like, were still foreign to Myles. Even so the Basilica's exterior gripped his attention—those yellow bricks turning white under the heat of the sun, the tallest steeple shaped in a long cone topped with a cross flanked by a set of two conical steeples of different heights, both topped with smaller crosses. In the center reigned a heavy wooden double-door with sturdy black hinges, enclosed by a pointed arch with overlapping pleats.

Myles approached the door to see the grains beneath the aged burnishing. He traced his fingers along the largest grain that looked like an eye watching who was coming into the church. A crack outlined this eye.

Myles pulled the right door-panel. The door made no noise—it was unlocked. He opened it further. No electronic lights were on. The light came into the chamber through colorful stained-glass pictures on both sides of the wall: they depicted saints. He could not clearly see the figures, but their color combinations mesmerized him. He stepped inside the door and closed it behind him. He narrowed his eyes; the stained-glass pictures blurred, turning kaleidoscopic. He crept to the leftmost corner of the last pew. Sitting in this solemn place of worship, he heard his own shapeless voice within:

Were we created after God's own image?

Myles had no idea why this thought came to him. *Does God look like me? Or do I look like God?* He shook, suddenly: "How shameless," he heard his own whisper. When he was a toddler, Myles understood that attending church with mother was a sensible weekend routine. He embraced the stories of Christ's birth, of the creation of the world, and of Adam and Eve. They were no more different than children's stories he had read: *Peter Pan, The Secret Garden, Black Beauty*, and the like. Myles loved these stories. But he had no recollection of believing them.

Myles's brain began to hurt. He rubbed his eyes hard. The cool air, suspended among the high pillars that vaulted the ceiling, felt getting chilly, and indifferent. The tabernacle tower on the altar stood still, giving out its metallic luster.

Outside, the sun was bright and warm. Yet Myles sensed the cool air that had seeped into his skin in the Basilica. No thoughts to focus on, he squatted on the concrete edge that protected the flowerbed full of canna lilies—red and yellow.

Tyrone came out of the administration building and, loosening his striped tie, squatted by Myles.

"All went well," Tyrone said before Myles had asked him anything.

Tyrone was telling the truth, Myles was certain—Tyrone's right eye emitted a bright ray of confidence and vigor: Tyrone was smiling, showing all his teeth.

"Congratulations, brother."

"Too soon for that, Myles." Tyrone threw a gaze at the top of the golden dome. "But I will know soon enough." He then patted Myles's back once as he had done when he was in good mood. "So where did you go while I was inside?"

"Oh, I just walked around. Real nice place. It would be great if you could come here, to this college."

Myles got up and touched a gigantic canna leaf that was swaying near his shoulder. He then peeled the leaf off the stalk. He waved the leaf at the direction of the Basilica building and the golden dome, not knowing why he was doing it.

Expulsion

"YOU LOOK WELL, Mr. Odam." A nun in her habit, who stood about six feet, stopped outside Room 220. She was making her rounds, pushing a book cart. "Would you care for some books this morning?"

"Sister Brianne. Thank you." Aware that she was speaking to Tyrone, Myles responded. "Tyrone is sedated."

"Oh, I am terribly sorry, Myles." Vocalizing each word with exaggerated lip movement, she goggled and stretched her back as if she was about to step back.

"Just a routine procedure, Sister."

"God bless him. He's such a wonderful gentleman." She then picked up a few magazines. "Do you think he might like something to read later?"

"Maybe tomorrow, Sister."

"All right. Tell Tyrone I said hi, will you please?"

"Certainly."

The squeaking of the book cart diminished with Sister Brianne.

Tyrone raised his head.

"Good job, brother. I owe you for that."

"She means well."

"I know. But if I respond to her, she comes in here and plops down in the chair and yaks, yaks, yaks ... By the time she is done, I'm dead."

"Why don't you keep the door closed around this time. Every day. She might get the idea."

"She won't. Love thy neighbor—you know."

"Nuns choose to be that way, I think."

"I'm not good with Bible bangers, really."

"Those are the Evangelicals—Tyrone. She's Catholic."

"Whatever ..."

"I know you've never had good luck with nuns—I mean since we were in our teens."

"My high-school days were miserable, I tell you." Tyrone shook his head. "How can I forget them."

"Yeah, I remember Sister Marguerita—a real hard-boiled egg."

"I couldn't take those Bible discussions every other Friday morning in the auditorium. Recitation, explanation, and then discussion—that's how she put together her class."

"Sister Maggie presiding over it all."

"Yeah, Sister Maggie's Bible Hour," Tyrone said, chuckling.

Tyrone took the sponge out of the ice water and licked it. "It was required of all the tenth, eleventh, and twelfth graders. I gave her a hard time, every time. She had to get back at me—you know, revenge. By treating me like a piece of crap in public."

"She did a pretty good job of that."

"She sure did. She kicked me out of the school, brother."

"You were okay with that, weren't you?"

"I don't know." Tyrone picked up the remote and raised the head portion of his bed, straightened out his top sheet and blanket.

"You want to sleep for a while?"

"Yeah. I'm kind of tired."

"Sometimes medicines do that. You know—make you sleep." Myles stood by the windowsill, looked at the six red maples, and then laid himself on the cushion beneath the window. The ceiling was white. This fiberglass ceiling had no pattern: it was like an empty canvas waiting for color. Myles stared at the whiteness and let his mind drift.

❧

Six weeks remained in the 1973-1974 academic year. The aroma of early summer stemmed from the grassy ground surrounding the school, pervading under the bright sunlight.

Bible Discussion Class was one of the courses required of all senior high school pupils. Sister Marguerita, the principal of the school, held this class in the school's auditorium every other Friday. As she had done so at the beginning of every class, Sister Marguerita stood behind a music stand and glanced over her notes placed on the center of the stand. She remained motionless. No one could guess if she were praying, or preparing herself for speaking, or retrieving some allegories she had used months or even years earlier that she might be able to use for that day's discussion again. The hum of voices died away and the auditorium turned as still as a pond on a windless day. Her silence commanded the pupils.

She raised her head and stepped forward to the first row of her audience. There were sixteen pupils in the first row, the aisle dividing them into two groups of eight. With her sterling gray eyes, she brushed each pupil's gaze. Myles was sitting in the third row, on the left side of the aisle; and Tyrone in the second row, on the right side of the aisle. Her inscrutable eyes did not touch Myles: He was outside her radar.

"Believing," Sister Marguerita joined her palms at her breast and cast her gaze heavenward, "is the very foundation of faith." Thus began the session.

Is she playing a nun like in a movie? Is it a trance-like sacred ecstasy she is immersed in? Myles wondered about it, chasing his own imaginative speculations that emerged one after another. In the end his brain concluded nothing.

Myles had never viewed people of holy orders with suspicion. When Cecilia used to take him to the church every Sunday to hear Father Evans preach, Myles never questioned anything the priest said or why Myles went to church—his brain worked unreceptively about these things. One day his mother suddenly stopped going to church. She did not force Myles to attend Sunday services afterwards. Not only did Myles stop attending the church, but he stopped thinking about it all together: Father Evans; people in the congregation to whom Myles had to greet after the service; those quarterly bazaars for the poor and the needy; and Christmas gatherings such as plays and concerts. It was surprising to him that this detachment from church happened to him as if naturally, and no issues troubled him.

Tyrone had flatly refused when Cecilia initially decided her family should attend church service. He infuriated Grandmother Cora, not because he did not want to go to church but because he yelled at his mother to get lost.

"Don't try to be a mother all of a sudden," Tyrone said.

Grandmother Cora slapped him. As if by reflex, he made his right hand into a fist.

"Don't you dare!" Grandmother shouted.

Tyrone froze. But his right eye could burn her whole. Myles dashed out of the house in fear and did not return home until that evening, and then he slept on the couch. If Tyrone were still angry at mother and Grandmother Cora, he would have taken it out on Myles through verbal abuse or by a deadly uppercut or two at his jaw.

While Sister Marguerita continued her lecture, Myles kept his eyes down on the waxed floor that peeked out between his bowlegged knees. Her voice passed over Myles's head—a low vocal range vibrating the air of the auditorium scented by the incense from the thurible. The first twenty minutes of the session ended sooner than Myles had expected. It was now time for Questions and Answers.

A high-pitched voice made Myles looked back. Four rows behind stood a mature girl with thick blond hair cut unevenly at her shoulder.

"I realize that, without believing, faith does not exist. How can I believe that the words in the Bible are of God's? Is it wrong of me to assume that those words were written by human beings in ancient times, so they are a human creation?"

The questioner maintained her eyes fixed on Sister Marguerita. The girl must be a senior, getting ready to graduate to go to college. She remained erect, and fearless.

"God created us in His image. This means He possesses all human qualities we have. This means also that what is ours belongs to Him. And we are all endowed with God's attributes. God and we are one entity, Miss Sophia Hollander. Therefore, it is not strange to say that what human beings have written belongs to Him as well."

"Thank you, Sister Marguerita."

Another student rose to pose a challenge.

"I reckon the phrase, 'God created us in His image,' comes from Genesis in the Old Testament," Marvin Fisher, the first-base player in the Blessed Mary baseball team, said. "Genesis must have been written down by somebody, as Sophia has just pointed out. Since, according to your teaching, God and we are one, do you think it is correct to say: Although this phrase was written by human being, God also communicated it to the writer of this phrase?"

He cleared his throat.

"The answer to your question, Mr. Fisher, is 'yes,' only so far as you *believe* in the oneness of God and us." Sister Marguerita emphasized the word *believe*, opening her lips and showing the tip of her tongue touching the back of her front teeth.

A female voice came from somewhere in the back, but Myles could not see her from the third row where he was.

"Did anyone witness God dictating the phrase to the writer of Genesis? If yes, Sister Marguerita, who would that witness be—what is his or her name?"

"Christian faith presupposes the will to believe on the part of the holder of that faith. The verb 'to presuppose' means: 'to require' or 'to entail.' So, before identifying the writer of this phrase and discovering the circumstances in which the phrase had come about, you begin with believing in the phrase, Miss Susan—"

"Huang," Susan answered for Sister Marguerita. "But—"

"Yes, Miss Susan Huang."

"Well, thank you for your answer."

Susan's voice was soft, but a touch of detachment could be felt, which echoed in silence.

"Sister Marguerita," A thick throaty voice familiar to Myles called out. It was Tyrone—his big body occupying a space near the music stand, his left foot sticking out to the aisle. "What about the birth of Christ?"

"Yes?"

"The Bible says Christ was born without Joseph and Mary making love. They have a special word for it—is it the 'Virgin Birth of Christ' or something? How can anyone be born without male-female intercourse? Without male ejaculation into a female's vagina? Am I to believe in this far-out story, Sister?"

"No one has forced you to believe it, Tyrone Odam. But you've been a student here at Blessed Mary's School that runs on Christian credo."

"A credo that has us believe something that has no realistic basis."

She stepped forward and stood facing Tyrone.

"Sister, have you ever loved a man?"

"Totally irrelevant! The word 'atheist' describes people like you,"

Sister Marguerita said in a gruff voice, her gray eyes glacial. "Don't you commit blasphemy in this sacred place, Tyrone." She slapped Tyrone in the face. "This will chase the devil out of you."

The whole assembly gasped and stood up, leaning forward.

At once, Tyrone's right hand slashed the air like a flash of lightning and landed on Sister Marguerita's left jaw below the ear which threw her head back. She reached for the music stand, stumbled half-circle, and hit the floor with her left shoulder. Her lecture notes flew about.

"I have the right to speak what I think!"

"Leave this school immediately, Tyrone Odam!" She rose and showed the door in the back of the auditorium.

"Gladly," Tyrone said, his fisted hands trembling. "You quack!" he yelled as he stormed from the hall.

❧

Josephine said nothing to Tyrone the day after he had been expelled from Blessed Mary. Myles suspected that she was waiting for Tyrone to come to her to talk about his troubles. She did not probe Myles for what happened, either. She stayed distant, both from Tyrone and from Myles. Her silent treatment irritated Myles—he had not caused her to steer clear of him, except for the possibility that he had said nothing to her about Tyrone's outburst that shook the entire school. Josephine must have known about the expulsion because, when it happened, she had been in the church kitchen with her food service team—Sister Marguerita had to have reported her decision on Tyrone immediately to Father Evans who, in turn, would have related it to Josephine in the kitchen. Tyrone must have known this chain of events would occur—he asked Josephine if he could talk to her.

"Of course. Let's sit down." Josephine was quick. They headed for the living room. "Myles, you join us."

Myles followed them into the living room and sat sideway on the couch arm and held against his stomach a beige square pillow that Josephine must have sewn years before.

"I know you've heard, Auntie Jo. About my expulsion from Blessed Mary."

"I'm glad you feel free to talk about it."

"I didn't at first."

"But you knew I knew—I'm sure."

"I'm so sorry it happened."

Myles could not believe Tyrone had possessed such an unaffected apologetic tone.

"I disapprove of your hitting Sister Marguerita and calling her a quack. You have all the reasons in the world to be expelled from the school. But …" She folded her arms and cast her gaze directly at Tyrone's forehead. "I support you on expressing your own thoughts. And I applaud you for your courage to take your own stand on your religious view. Not everyone can do it."

"So, you know why I never felt comfortable going to church and mingling with church people."

"Of course, I do." With her palm, she rubbed her upper chest. "What happened has happened, Tyrone—and we need not dwell on it. I want to talk about what you are going to do from this point on. Do you have any thoughts you want to discuss?"

"I want to go to Philadelphia—to the place you mentioned a while ago."

"Mount Olive Boarding School for Boys?"

Tyrone nodded. His right eye shone with determination, and his lips tightened.

"It's another Christian school, you know that?"

"I do."

"Can you handle it? I mean you have to live by a strict set of conduct rules, not necessarily Christian rules, but common-sense rules of human interaction."

"I can, Auntie."

"Okay. First, you have to pass the transfer exam and get accepted."

"I will do that."

"Suppose you pass. The school begins in the second half of August. We have two and half months. How will you spend your time?"

"I looked at the newspaper—the classified section. Two 7-Elevens are looking for high school kids to do their food services and cashier work during the summer."

"In Mishawaka?"

"No. In South Bend."

"How would you go back and forth every day?"

"By bus. It only takes fifteen minutes as you know."

"Good plan, Tyrone. I am here for you, always … you know that."
Josephine stood up.

He's made up his mind—he will never change it. Myles was certain.
His gaze followed Tyrone ascending the staircase to his room.

"Tyrone," Myles said.

Tyrone's back faced Myles.

Is this it, Tyrone? Come August we will be separated. The palms of
Myles's hands broke out in sweat.

Spying

It DID NOT devastate Myles, but it stunned him—the size of Tyrone's penis. The shaft had shrunk into his pubic hair, like the bellows of an accordion. Only the glans, with its pinkish luster faded into beige, peeked out of his groin.

"Oh, brother, why are you staring at my dick?"

"Jesus—"

Nurse Joyce burst out laughing. "This is your brother, Myles. Didn't you guys shower together when you were kids?

"Sure, we did," Tyrone said.

Joyce covered Tyrone's penis with a towel and continued to bathe his arms, neck, and chest with a damp cloth. She had already finished his legs.

"If you don't use your body, it atrophies."

"Your thing doesn't go waste. It's hibernating." Myles's matter-of-fact tone sounded un-Myles. "You had good use of it all your life, Tyrone."

"I guess I did."

"Sophia Hollander. She was your first, wasn't she?"

"But I wasn't her first—I tell you that."

"Brothers, please." Joyce stopped washing Tyrone, feigning peevishness, with her hands on her hips.

"Sorry, Joyce."

Shaking her head, she got back to wiping Tyrone's toes.

My God, he sounds just like he's talking to his ex-wife. Myles stood like a log. He then grinned, silently mocking at Joyce.

"How do you know about Sophia and me?" Tyrone muted his voice. "Man, that's a long time ago. I was seventeen, kicked out of Blessed Mary."

"I saw you two. You were at it."

"Okay, done," Joyce said, negating what she thought she heard. She emptied the washing bowl at the sink in the bathroom and wrung the towel hard. With the bowl and towel, Joyce marched right out of the door.

One day in late June of 1974, a few weeks after Blessed Mary had completed its graduation ceremony, the rubbing of clothes as faint as the buzzing of a mosquito stopped Myles as he stepped inside the kitchen backdoor. Somebody was in the house. Tyrone had gone to South Bend to 7-Eleven where he worked as a part-timer. Josephine was in Chicago all day for a religious convention, leading the kitchen service team of the Blessed Mary church. Myles had just returned from his solitary bicycle excursion to the wooded hill on the outskirts of Mishawaka—his favorite thing to do in his spare time. The foliage was like a gigantic blanket when Myles lay on dead leaves, and the sunrays penetrated through the trees like countless spotlight beams onstage.

Myles stood leaning against the sink. Clothes were not the only source of the noise. Someone was moaning: heavy breathing mixed with quivering that sounded as if belched from deep in the stomach. Myles got closer to the inside door leading into the living room. The noise was coming from there. He opened the living room door, suppressing the noise of the door handle.

Two figures entwined on the couch in an irregular circular motion. Tyrone's thick legs were exposed all the way down to his ankles, and a girl was squatting on Tyrone's groin and kept her circular motion with her hips, clinging on to his neck—and Tyrone's arms encircling her back. Her summer one-piece blanketed it all.

Oh my god! Myles almost yelled, but quickly covered his mouth.

The girl looked around. Tyrone hugged her back against his chest and started his hip motion, his eyes closed.

"No, no. Stop."

"Yes, come on."

Wasn't that what infuriated Tyrone a few years back? So much so that he drove a burning stove poker right into the butt cheek of Clem McCullum when he was mounting their mother? Clem must have been doing to her what Tyrone was doing with this girl now. The thing was that the lady visitor did not let out desperate moan as Cecilia had. Nothing seemed to exist for the lady visitor—she was deeply into her body rubbing with Tyrone. From the cracked kitchen door, Myles could only see her back. Then, it dawned on him: a blond girl with her hair unevenly cut at the shoulder. Yes, she had asked Sister Marguerita the first question in that Bible Studies session: Sophia Hollander. She had graduated from Blessed Mary a month after Tyrone's expulsion.

Myles had never given any thought to Tyrone's interest in this blond girl—it never occurred to him Tyrone would be charmed by a brainy girl like Sophia. When he came to think of it, Myles did remember seeing from his classroom on the second floor Tyrone and a blond girl in the playground a few times. They seemed to keep distant from each other. Myles hardly thought that they were more than just friends—boys and girls did talk for whatever the reason. Myles probably was the only one who could talk to neither girls nor to boys. They had decided that he was mostly mute, but noticed his occasional rattling voice with its strange vibrations. Myles did not stutter but he had a hard time spitting out words: his brain and throat did not communicate well. With all this, it was out of the question that Myles would get close to girls, nor even to boys for that matter. Often, he wished he were a class clown who could make fun of himself and laugh out loud with them. But he even lacked this skill—he just could not learn how. Myles dreamed of acceptance, but believed it unthinkable.

Why did Sophia visit now, for the first time? Did she know Tyrone had only a few weeks before his departure for Philadelphia? Did Tyrone take a day off from work knowing Josephine would be away and Myles would be out bicycling? Did Sophia and Tyrone like each other, and nobody knew it? Something was going on under Sophia's skirt while Tyrone closed his eyes and shared long kisses with her. Was this what the boys called "losing their virginity"?

My God, I would never lose my virginity because I don't know how to start a talk with a girl I like. Myles's chest burned.

Noiselessly closing the kitchen door, Myles let himself out through the backdoor. The three maple trees luxuriated under Tyrone's window. Of the two green-leafed maples flanking the red-leafed Bloodgood, one on the left had grown thicker than the other. The branches of the Bloodgood maple had firmed up with astringent luster.

Myles waited out here until he heard the front door squeak and shut. A car engine ignited, then its combustion faded.

❧

"I got paid, Myles."

"You got paid before. You get paid every week. What's so special about today?"

"Auntie will be late tonight. She left a message to take you out to dinner. So, we are eating out together."

"You? Taking me out?" Myles sat up in Josephine's armchair by the couch, facing Tyrone.

"Sure. What's the big deal?"

"I can't believe it."

"Don't argue with me, Little One."

"Don't call me 'Little One'. I'm almost as tall as you are."

"Whatever ..." Tyrone fixed his shoelaces. "C'mon. We're going for Chinese."

The boys left the house and headed to the Chinese restaurant near the Greyhound terminal.

"I bet they don't have curry veggie lo mein."

"Never heard of it."

"It's one of Auntie Jo's recipes."

"Maybe she got it from somebody. She cooks it for those people?"

"Sometimes. There are a few packs left in the freezer."

At China Pearl, Tyrone ordered a pork/chicken/shrimp combination on a bed of steamed vegetables, and Myles opted for a dish of steamed whole perch with sliced ginger and spring onion scattered on top. Tyrone's plate was two sizes larger than Myles's, yet it looked like an ordinary Chinese dish.

"How is it?" Tyrone asked.

"It's very soft." Myles scooped two more forkful of fish meat. "So, how was it?" Myles caught indifference in his own voice—he must have been thinking of Tyrone and Sophia on the couch. Myles had promised himself never to sit in that couch again.

"What?"

"I meant, your big dish."

Myles's heart pounded, hating Tyrone's brazen pretention. Was Myles defeated by Tyrone's refusal to share with him what happened that early afternoon with Sophia? Or was Myles upset that he was still a virgin and Tyrone was no longer? Did Sophia divide these siblings in less than half hour? If this were true, Myles would have blamed Tyrone for letting her do it to them. On second thought, Myles could settle on the fact that Tyrone simply had done what he had to do as a man. It was the time for Tyrone to do it, perhaps. Myles's body signals were not yet strong enough: Tyrone's apparently were.

"You don't really chew it, do you?" Myles asked.

"Too much chewing spoils the meat taste."

Myles smirked. But at once he swallowed his smirk: violence in public might put Tyrone in jail if he blew up at Myles. Myles did not want that. Tyrone was about to venture out to the east coast where future, however it might be, awaited him.

"The shrimp tastes stronger than the rest. There's not much pork flavor."

"How was work today, brother?" Myles did not raise his face, but he sensed Tyrone's head moving away from the plate—he was staring at Myles. These words just popped out of his mouth.

"Why do you ask? That was never your concern before."

"I don't know. It's my concern now."

"Man, you're talking a lot today. Already enough for the entire year."

"Don't you feel good when your mute brother talks?"

"Sure. But you know what—you can be a mean son-of-a-bitch."

Here, knowing Tyrone was not in a violent mood, Myles let his smirking come back. Myles too was surprised how many words had come out of his mouth since Tyrone came home, and how many words he had to suppress for the fear of him blowing up at him.

"Auntie Jo will be happy to hear me talk. She will hug me." Myles was scooping fish into his mouth but was not swallowing it down quick enough.

"She is a real hugger, you know?"

Myles wondered what Josephine would say when she had found out that Tyrone and Sophia made love on the couch. Would she say: "Men folks are supposed to do that," or "Never before marriage—Tyrone should go to church and confess." Tyrone would never hit Josephine like he had done Sister Marguerita. The nun's high-handed condescension had agitated Tyrone, Myles was certain. Josephine had none of that. With all his rough "I don't care" attitude, Tyrone still loved his aunt. Myles had seen him letting her kiss him on his cheek.

A tiny bone pricked Myles's left tonsil. He cleared his throat and then coughed. When he threw some ginger and spring onions in his mouth and chewed well, these veggies scraped the bone off his tonsil and pushed it down. A glass of water cooled his agitated tonsil.

Having finished his three-meat combination, Tyrone ordered a dish of Singapore noodles. And he used a pair of chopsticks.

"Where did you learn how to do that?"

"What, eat noodles?"

"Use chopsticks."

"From a Chinese woman at work."

"You learn quick."

"Some things I can do pretty well."

You should add a new skillset to that, Tyrone: how to get ecstatic moans out of girls.

Myles had to face the truth: he was jealous of Tyrone because he was not a virgin boy anymore. Myles was envious of Tyrone because he could keep a man's secret to himself. How Myles wanted Tyrone to come to him on his own and tell him all about his ecstatic loss of his virginity. Myles would have felt closer to him had he brought one of Sophia's friends home so that Myles could make love to her in his locked room upstairs. She would do what Tyrone had brought Sophia to the house for: To take his virginity.

While he was trying to scoop the last piece of his fish with a fork, Myles sensed a hard tingling in his groin. Myles wanted so badly to be a man—like Tyrone.

Graduation

Dr. Canon had suggested to Myles that it would be in his best interest to make financial arrangements as soon as Myles had the legal power to do so. Tyrone had appointed Myles as his executor of his will, his power of attorney, and his healthcare representative. Myles himself had been ambivalent about taking steps to alter their independent financial setups. Dr. Canon must have spoken to Tyrone about this issue— Tyrone had urged Myles, from time to time, to let him transfer all but four hundred dollars from his bank account to Myles's.

Does he know something I don't?

Myles had been suspecting Tyrone for some time in fear of left behind alone. But to get the truth out of Tyrone seemed to mean he would be asking Tyrone to estimate the month of his death. Tyrone should have left the hospital by now, but his stay continued because of his C. diff infection. He was still in isolation and was on antibiotic therapy. He had discontinued his rehabilitation exercises—the infection had depleted his strength. Myles was concerned that pneumonia might set in any time. Tyrone's immunity had weakened and he could no longer walk around with a cane in his room, gazing at the red maples from the window, taking a shower daily on his own. Nowadays, he was on catheter, on both ends.

A few days before, Dr. Canon had come in to see Tyrone—a routine visit. While examining Tyrone, she took his right arm and, with her fingers, traced his blood vessels: up toward his elbow joint and down toward his wrist—and repeating it. Her eyes focused on his arm, but Myles could tell her brain was turning.

"Anything wrong, Doctor?" Myles asked.

"I was just thinking. Would you be interested in learning the basics of nursing?"

"May I ask what you mean?"

"Certainly. You learn simple things like cleaning him, giving him Jevity through the J-tube, crushing his meds and injecting them into the tube, changing his sheets and underpad."

"Absolutely."

"Tyrone will be happy to have you around 24/7 as his caregiver."

"Actually, I've been doing something like caregiving. So, I'm used to it."

"Good. I'll assign a nurse as your instructor. You will learn quickly, I know."

"He'll be okay," Tyrone said.

Dr. Canon patted Tyrone's hand and smiled at him. "I cannot estimate exactly when, but you may be able to go home soon. Myles will be your nurse."

The following day, the day-nurse supervisor brought in a middle-aged nurse. "Varsha Gokhale. She will coach you on nursing basics. She's been with Memorial for eight years now. Well experienced. You'll like her."

"How do you do?" Varsha said.

Myles at once detected a foreign accent in her speech—the kind of sound a cupped tongue would make.

"I'm originally from India, as you have noticed."

Myles liked her distant demeanor that came with a gentle yet straight dark gaze.

"Nice to meet you, Miss … Go-khá-le."

"You may call me Varsha."

"Hello, Varsha."

It was Tyrone. He was looking at Varsha and Myles.

"Oh, hello Mr. Odam. How are you feeling today? I substituted for Joyce twice before so we kind of know each other, don't we?"

"I feel better, thank you." Tyrone pulled his blanket up to his shoulders and turned toward the window.

"Mr. Odam, may I please lift your blanket, to see your hip area? I think I have just the right exercise for your caregiver to try."

Myles detected a peculiar odor which Varsha must have sensed several seconds ago. This odor was not entirely foreign to Myles. It was the smell of C. diff. Before, whenever he smelled it, Myles would press the buzzer to call the nurse—whoever was in the nurse's station. Now Myles was the one to clean up the leakage from Tyrone's rectal catheter under the supervision of Varsha.

Myles stepped over to the shelf by the door which contained boxes of three different sizes of surgical gloves colored purple, blue, or yellow. Myles threw out the old gloves he had had to put on when he arrived at Room 220. He picked a blue pair—a medium size that covered his hands comfortably.

"Raise your knees a little, Tyrone," Myles said in a matter-of-fact tone.

He then took a stack of soft non-toilet tissue and gently wiped the leakage: It took four wipes. Then he sprayed the area with Proshield Foam & Spray.

"Now, Myles," Varsha said while holding Tyrone's bent knees. "The anti-rash cream must be distributed evenly over the area."

Myles felt squeamish pulling up Tyrone's large testicles, to apply the anti-rash cream underneath.

Good god, his balls are disproportionately bigger than his penis, Myles observed.

"Just do your job, Mr. Caregiver." Tyrone said. "There's nothing to inspect."

The anti-rash ointment had a hard oily base to it: It took Myles a few minutes to spread it evenly.

"Now, Myles, the underpad next."

"Let me see if I can do it."

Myles turned Tyrone rightward so that he was on his side, gripping the siderail of the bed with his hands. Myles rolled away the stained underpad, pushing it under Tyrone's body. He then spread a clean underpad, squeezed its top portion under the rolled-up underpad as far as he could thrust.

"Okay, Tyrone, turn the other way. And grab the siderail there."

Myles walked over to the other side of Tyrone's bed. He removed the stained rolled-up underpad from under Tyrone and then pulled the new pad toward himself. And gently he let Tyrone lay on his back on the clean pad.

"Good job, Myles. I can tell you've watched nurses closely. Just one thing, though: Next time, place the clean pad a bit higher so that his butt falls into a comfortable position."

"Yes, ma'am." Myles watched Varsha cover Tyrone with the blanket and wrap his feet together with it, also. "Do I need to take his vitals now?"

"At five. I'll come around then."

Varsha left the room.

Tyrone was already dozing, with his breathing slightly snorty.

Myles thought of calling Varsha back. But then the snorty breathing was not necessarily a sign of a breathing problem, Myles reasoned. He discarded his blue gloves and put on a new pair of yellow gloves. Then he stretched himself out on the cushion below the window.

❧

In early May of 1975, Tyrone, then eighteen years old, graduated from Mount Olive Boarding School for Boys in Philadelphia. The parents, the siblings, the relatives of those young graduates filled the gymnasium where the graduation ceremony took place. The graduates in their black gowns with golden crosses stitched onto their right chest seated themselves on the stage. Halfway into the ceremony, the master of ceremonies called Tyrone's name. This announcement caught Myles off guard. Myles stretched his neck in anticipation of what was going to happen on stage.

Please, Tyrone, don't say anything wacky—like "God does not exist, but this planet keeps rotating."

Tyrone stood up: dignified and imposing. He paused, stepped forward to the podium. His right eye grazed over the audience from right to left. He repositioned the microphone in front of him. After several seconds of calculated silence, Tyrone spoke of what Mount Olive had given him, of searing high into the boundless expanse of freedom that, in turn, stipulated responsibility for one's action, and of his ambition to succeed in the field of medical technology. At the close of his address, he cast his eye upon Josephine who was sitting in the first row in the seat closest to the aisle.

"I owe much to Josephine Floden, my mother." Tyrone gestured her to stand up to take a bow. "And to my little brother, Myles."

Why does he have to add "little"? Why can't I simply be his "brother"?

Both Josephine and Myles stood up, turned around, and bowed to the audience. Myles followed Josephine, not knowing why he was bowing to them. The applauding audience's gentle faces huddled together in a veiled blurriness of curiosity. This was the first time in the sixteen years of his life that Myles had heard Tyrone address someone as "mother," in a heartfelt tone Myles had never known that Tyrone possessed. Turning back to the stage, Myles caught a glimpse of Tyrone smirking at him—that was his big brother he had always known.

Josephine seemed unmoved, or she was restraining herself not to make a scene. Myles assumed Tyrone's weighty voice addressing her as his "mother" resonated in her heart more than anything else that had gone before in her life. He could be wrong, though.

After the ceremony, during the refreshment hour, Tyrone was already talking about his admittance to Rutgers University and about taking two required courses during the summer. His vocal pitch rose when he told them that he would be commuting to the university's Camden campus in South Jersey across from Philadelphia. And his pitch rose yet higher and louder with pride when he shared with them that, since he would have a studio apartment in downtown, he would be working at a coffee shop called "Sasha" at Twelfth and Chestnut Streets at night from six to eleven-thirty.

Frankly, Tyrone's enthusiasm for new plans sounded like a fabrication of some sort to Myles. But it was happening. A brother of Myles's who, throughout his whole life, had stayed away from academic studies, teachers, even from his classmates. Now he could not wait to plunge into a new college life on the east coast. A few years before, this had been but a dream of his which could have evaporated by the time he turned eighteen. The dream had materialized: the boldest decision and change of his youth. There had to be something that had steered him into this direction. Josephine had helped open doors for Tyrone, for sure. But Myles had suspected Tyrone might have had a mentor who could guide him and nurture in him the will and the motivation to face the new path and step forward onto it. The taming of a wild black wolf, intelligent, independent, yet deeply wounded—this image flitted by behind Myles's eyes.

At two o'clock, the event came to its close. Families dispersed in all directions where their cars were waiting for them. Josephine, Tyrone, and Myles walked to the then-renowned seafood restaurant Bookbinder's located on Fifteenth Street between Walnut and Locust.

Entering the restaurant, Myles froze on the spot: Josephine went straight to the reserved table in the back, ignoring Tyrone. This was the first time Myles had ever heard the aggressive tick-tocks her low-heel shoes made. Tyrone slowed down and tilted his head left to read Josephine's face. Myles thought she looked like a ceramic mask, with not even an ounce of warmth.

What's the matter with her? Myles wondered.

"Sit down, boys." Josephine was already glancing through the menu.

Tyrone shot a skewed gaze at Myles and then at Josephine who was now ordering a lobster dish for Myles and another for herself. "What are you having, Tyrone?"

"Uh, do they have branzino?"

"Sure, they do. It's listed right here at the top of the Mediterranean cuisine section."

"I'd like the fish."

Myles abruptly turned to Tyrone who was staring at Josephine. Tyrone's slightly frowned face, his stooped posture with his elbows on the table hinted to Myles that Tyrone did not grasp what was going on with Josephine. Myles knew Tyrone would wait until Josephine had initiated the dialogue.

⁂

After their quiet seafood dinner, they all walked on Fifteenth Street towards Market. The Greyhound terminal located underground there in the concourse.

Tyrone hugged Myles tight, and Myles gave Tyrone an equally hard hug back.

Josephine stepped back when Tyrone extended his arms.

"What was that, Tyrone? That little show on stage?"

"What are you talking about?" Tyrone's right eye darkened, pleading.

"Auntie-Jo—" Myles touched Josephine's arm, which she gently slipped away from.

"I am not your mother, Tyrone. I am your aunt. The Family Court designated me as your surrogate mother—a guardian, in other words."

"I know that." Tyrone put his head a little to the right as if getting a better view of Josephine's face. "More than anybody else."

"By calling me 'mother,' you made yourself look so devoted to your parent. What an actor."

"But—"

"But what?" Josephine cast a piercing gaze at Tyrone. "I wanted to see the boy I've known so well for years—unadorned, unfeigned."

The speaker blasted the announcement on the departure of the bus to South Bend. It shook the concourse with its blurred dissonance.

Josephine picked up her suitcase and suspended her belted-handbag over her left shoulder. "Good-bye, Tyrone."

Myles hugged Tyrone once again; Tyrone did not respond.

"Safe trip home," Tyrone said, choked.

At the gate, Myles looked back.

Tyrone had not moved. He raised his hand high and showed its palm at Myles. And then he walked backward, now waving his large hand. And, finally, Tyrone turned around toward the escalator to exit the terminal onto the street level.

❧

Two hours of smooth and monotonous Greyhound bus ride later, Josephine and Myles arrived at Harrisburg, the capital of Pennsylvania one hundred and seven miles from downtown Philadelphia via I-76 West. The driver announced that the bus would depart Harrisburg in twenty minutes. Both Josephine and Myles got off the vehicle. She headed for the powder room. Myles walked straight to a small stall and bought a bottle of Coke and a can of peanuts. He sat on the bench right across from Gate 8 so that he could see other passengers would get on the bus in a while. Josephine bought a black coffee at the stall and came over to Myles's bench and sat down, careful not to spill the coffee that filled her cup to its rim. She sipped it, making noise. Myles must have been looking at her, she said: "Anything wrong?"

"Are you happy he graduated?"

"Yes. And I am proud of him—you know why he spoke before all those people?"

"Because he is an atheist?"

"No, not because he is an atheist. But he is summa cum laude—of his graduating class."

"If you are happy he graduated, why were you mean to him at the terminal? You two should have hugged goodbye. But you didn't."

"You heard me when I was talking to him. I don't know Tyrone the sophisticated and worldly. I wanted back the kind of Tyrone I knew and loved, Myles."

"I think you were too harsh on him. He was confused. He called you 'mother' to please you, Auntie."

"That's exactly what gave me chills. I'd have been happy if he treated me as his aunt that I have been all those years."

"I hope you didn't hurt him."

Myles could not get a grip on Josephine's silence.

An announcement from Gate 8 followed the loud bell broken into five short metallic spurts. Passengers got on the bus. Josephine continued to sip her coffee as she neared the open entrance of the bus and Myles followed her, munching on his peanuts.

About five minutes later, the lights inside the bus went off. And the vehicle steered toward the exit and into the golden dusk. Empty seats scattered about, so did the passengers—each occupying two connected seats. Josephine too decided to take two seats on the other side of the aisle from Myles, to lay down to sleep. Myles took a seat in the back by the lavatory.

Once they were on the highway westward, the engine put out a steady pitch. Myles got sucked into the pitch. It grew hypnotizing. He liked this false sense of being sucked into a dark tunnel with no end.

There in the darkness, his memory resurrected in slow motion like a series of photos the graduation ceremony and how Tyrone played his part as a student of the highest honor. Myles wondered how much he had practiced his speech—for a week or two, perhaps, making notes all over his speech draft in red: certain words to emphasize, others to soften, adding silence here and there, marking when to provide effective exclamations, among other. Myles was hearing Tyrone's low-pitched intonation stemmed from his naturally thick voice. How Tyrone had learned all this skill in one year since he transferred to Mount Olive, was beyond Myles. Myles could only imagine Tyrone had adapted to the culture of the east coast—its sophistication, its opportunities to nurture self-esteem and self-assurance that grew out of putting oneself in the center of information throughway. Maybe it was more like the east coast culture embraced him. Calling Josephine "mother" was part of this large scheme—maybe, Myles wondered.

In a way, Josephine had taught them a lot—like a mentor would. But then she had been more of a mother to them than a mentor. Since Tyrone and Myles went to live with her by the court order, they both had seen how distinct Josephine was from Grandmother Cora and her younger sister Cecilia, the boys' biological mother. By the time Tyrone graduated from high school, this difference had become so pronounced that they felt they no longer knew their mother. It hurt Myles to know Tyrone did not see his own mother in the audience at his graduation. Myles was sure Tyrone had looked around the gymnasium from the podium, just in case Cecilia might have arrived in Philadelphia to share her oldest son's memorable day. Tyrone received no congratulation card from her, no call either. Their mother's indifference stung deep into Tyrone's already wounded heart. Myles felt his pain.

The engine kept moaning in a steady pitch. Myles leaned his head against the window. Outside stretched a dark purple dome with no stars, only thin cracks of gray clouds notching it.

No, I won't go to Mount Olive like Tyrone did. Mishawaka is my home. I can get a night-shift job that doesn't force me to talk. And if Josephine needs me, I'm right there. Myles made up his mind.

Homecoming

MYLES HAD FOUND an unofficial way of administering Jevity, water, and liquified medications into Tyrone's intestine through the J-tube—not using the plunger of the syringe, but letting the liquid go down at its own pace. He was certain nurses knew this method, but they went through the proper way as they had been taught at nursing schools. The non-plunger method took longer than using the plunger, but Myles could see exactly where he was as far as the downward movement of the liquid. Tyrone took two cans of Jevity for every meal. The nutritional liquid was supposed to help Tyrone gain weight, but he had shown no signs of weight gain. It seemed to Myles that what Tyrone took through the J-tube came out through the catheter tube connected to the plastic bag hung under his bed. And the bag seemed always full—a color of moss on an ancient stone.

"Have you tasted Jevity?" Curiosity brightened Tyrone's right eye. "Just wondered."

"No. I don't know what this tastes like. I never thought of tasting it, until now." Myles poured a small amount of Jevity into a two-ounce cup and gave it to Tyrone. "You can't drink it. Just lick it and see."

"I can't tell." Tyrone moved his lips fast like a bird pecking on seeks.

"No taste?"

"No … I don't think. But—well, doesn't matter." Tyrone backed down on his pillow. "You've been so good to me, Myles."

Josephine, when she was in the intensive care unit at St. Bartholomew of Braga Hospital in South Bend, had said the same thing, in the same way—she died two days later. During her last week on this planet, she talked about Tyrone. Tyrone had not come home since he'd graduated from Mount Olive High years before. She had kept saying she loved that rough nephew of hers and thought often of visiting him but did not: she feared her presence might cause a rekindling of dependence in him. She did not attend Tyrone's wedding to Rita Conway whose marriage lasted only eleven years. And Tyrone did not go to Josephine's funeral at the Church of Blessed Mary.

Josephine had never forgotten Tyrone's stunned right eye when, at the Greyhound terminal in Philadelphia, she told him she was not his mother and that he was faking his speech. She continually said to Myles she had to spurn Tyrone at that very moment to make him realize the direction he was heading for—she had seen his natural blatantness, nakedness fading away at that early age of eighteen. Josephine departed without letting Tyrone know her side of the story. Myles was not about to tell him her story—it was not Myles's place to step in on Josephine's behalf. Myles did not view himself as a middleman.

In mid-afternoon, that day, the window started to clatter. The sun cast its warmth on the floor, its brilliance lacking; despite it was July the first—a summer day. Myles stepped over to the window. The six red maples along the path into the wooded park tossed about in the gust.

Soon the dark cloud will hide the sun and drop a downpour of rain, Myles muttered and turned to Tyrone, motionless on the bed.

⸲

The telephone rang.

Myles picked up the receiver.

"May I speak to Myles Odam?"

Her voice penetrated his ear before Myles identified himself. "This is he."

"I am Janet Roberts from Human Registry. Memorial Hospital called us about your brother's wish to donate his body for research."

"Oh, I see. Which university is he going to?"

"He may remain there at Memorial, since it's a training hospital."

"I see."

"Your brother's death certificate states he died of cardiopulmonary arrest."

"That is correct."

"May I ask if your brother had any indications other than cardiopulmonary conditions? Within the three months prior to his demise."

"He suffered from sciatica, aspiration pneumonia, dysphasia ... and—"

"Mr. Odam?" Empathy replaced dominance in her voice. "I am so sorry."

"And Tyrone had C. diff."

"Oh, dear. How did he get it?"

"While in Memorial."

Myles heard a sigh escaping from her nose. Silence persisted. He volunteered no further information.

"We have a problem, Mr. Odam." She paused. "We are unable to accept your brother's body as he had planned."

"Because of the C. diff?"

"Yes. I am afraid so. Our protocols forbid us from accepting any bodies which had active infectious diseases. It's purely a safety issue."

Hot mucus filled Myles's nostrils and blocked the air. Tyrone was no longer here to tell him what to do.

"My deepest condolences, Mr. Odam." Her telephone clicked.

Myles placed the receiver back into the handset.

*

"How do you know the man you retrieve from the hospital is my brother, Mr. Donahue?" Myles's voice quivered during his call to Donahue Funeral Home on King's Highway. The harder Myles hid his fear of Tyrone extinguishing in flame, the more pronounced the quiver in his voice.

"I understand," Mr. Donahue, the director of the funeral home, said. "Each resting person in the hospital morgue carries an identification number and vital data. If you like, why don't you meet me at the hospital when I transfer your brother? You may verify him, then. I will give you a call when Mr. Odam has returned from the crematory in Collingswood, which probably will be about five-thirty this evening. You may stop by to receive his ashes, then."

"Yes, I will meet you at the hospital, Mr. Donahue."

"Not a problem, Myles."

As Donahue had suggested on the phone, Myles revisited Memorial Hospital—this time, the basement where the morgue was located. On the foyer was a zipped turquoise bag placed on a gurney, waiting for Myles's verification. The body inside the bag was, no doubt, Tyrone.

Despite being ill for more than two years he had maintained his sturdy bone structure: a mutation in Myles's family—as Josephine used to say. Tyrone was the only one in the family who graduated college, on his own. He was a mutation in this respect, also.

Ian, Donahue's assistant in a white medical coat, unzipped one third of the bag and opened the hems outward to show the person inside. Myles's lips and jaw tightened, and his nasal bone ached as he blocked tears. His right hand covered his mouth.

Myles stepped forward.

Ian stood before Myles with his arms stretched, shaking his head.

"Can't I touch him?"

"No, Mr. Odam. Not this time."

"He is my brother."

"Remember you opted for direct cremation. He has not been cleaned."

Tyrone's eyelids were closed but his eyeballs seemed slightly rolled up underneath his eyelids, his face ashen.

Ian's small left hand clasped the tip of the plastic bag, and his right fingers pulled the zipper back to the end of the thin zipper rail.

The closed turquoise bag laid on the gurney as if an iceberg broken off its main glacial mound, floating over the dark immense ocean, aimless.

Myles followed Donahue into his office in the funeral home, where he sat at a varnished desk with a landline phone on it. They faced each other across the desk. Myles handed him Tyrone's Last Will and Testament, which Donahue duplicated. He explained the cremation procedure in layperson's terms—short, plain. He then asked for 50% of the total cost previously quoted. Myles gave him his debit card.

"The rest should be paid when I claim him later, I suppose." Myles said.

"Yes, that is how it is." Donahue cast a quick stare at Myles over his rimless glasses and handed Myles's debit card and a yellow paper with some scribbles over to Ian who was waiting at the doorway.

Myles nodded to Ian. Ian threw a blank gaze at him from behind a pair of extra thick glasses which distorted his socketed eyes. Silent and inscrutable, Ian left the office with Myles's debit card.

"By the way, Myles, would you care to look at some of our urns for your brother?"

"Thank you, but I have another plan."

"Which is?"

"I am going to return his ashes to nature—to a forest in Mishawaka, Indiana."

"That's a beautiful idea. We have chauffeur services too if you'd like to use it."

"To Indiana?"

"Why not?"

"I'm fine, Mr. Donahue."

⁂

When Myles returned to Donahue's that evening, Tyrone was waiting for him on Donahue's desk—in a light cream-colored box, a box small enough Myles could hold it against his chest. After he paid the balance of Tyrone's cremation, Donahue opened the box and showed him Tyrone's pulverized ashes as fine as lime in a plastic bag. The box contained identification cards with cremation data on them. Donahue said these cards were required just in case Myles flew carrying him in his suitcase. Which Myles might very well be doing when going to Mishawaka in the coming summer.

"Is this all we are?"

"I'm afraid so. Just the calcium, Myles." Donahue fanned the cremation data cards on the palm of his left hand, then stacked them together, and put them back in the box. Ian was standing behind Donahue with an open plastic shopping bag with "Donahue Funeral Home—50 years of services in Cherry Hill, NJ." Donahue placed the box into the shopping bag and made a knot on top of the box. He drew a small cross on his chest with his right hand. He then nodded, with deference. Donahue and Myles shook hands. Ian could not be seen anywhere.

Myles got home at ten after six in the evening. His forty-minute visit to Donahue Funeral Home had felt more like two hours. Each minute seemed to have expanded twice, three times. His brain felt numbed since Dr. Canon confirmed that Tyrone had died in his sleep two days before. Myles spent the next day searching the Internet for a funeral home that would take on a simple cremation job. He found Donahue Funeral Home available to meet his specifications.

In the living room, Myles untied the funeral home bag, took the box out, and put it on the coffee table. The top shelf of Tyrone's entertainment center was empty. Myles could put Tyrone's ashes there. At first sight, the box seemed too tight for the space. But then, as he gave it a slight push, the box settled in its place, giving a narrow extra space in front of it. There Myles put a ten-inch wooden statue of the Virgin Mary. He had bought this statue the previous Christmas at Cherry Hill Mall as a gift to his neighbor. The salesclerk said that a Middle Eastern artist had carved it.

"Just this statue?" Myles asked.

"Everything you see here."

This statue never reached his neighbor: It stayed among winter socks in the top drawer of Tyrone's dresser.

The Bible was never part of Tyrone's library. Only when he had realized that his stroke back in May did not take away his speech, did he mention "God." Knowing all this, Myles still wanted to place the statue by Tyrone: My brother who came into this world without an identifiable father, only by the force of nature. A painful burning ignited in his brain.

Staring at the top shelf of the entertainment center where Tyrone resided now, Myles could not believe that this was all that remained of his brother. Until the day before yesterday he looked just like any male human—a congruent physical entity; and, in a matter of several hours, he had transformed into a boxful of calcium powder. But both were Tyrone.

Myles went to the bedroom and picked up his sleeping bag. The room suddenly turned hollow, and its ceiling higher. Myles had no resistance to the empty bedroom: he had gotten used to sleeping on the floor, bundled up in his sleeping bag. The sleeping bag, cushioned by the carpet, gave enough spongy comfort. But now he had no idea what to do with this apartment without Tyrone—Myles owned nothing except the sleeping bag. The television would go back to the entertainment center in the living room. And the unpainted wooden table, which was an organizer for Tyrone's medical supplies, would be folded and stored in the bedroom closet.

The wooden Virgin Mary on the shelf looked as if she cast her merciful gaze upon the cream-colored box. Yet, she seemed deeply in trance, alone, unaware of her surroundings. Had she always been a loner, destined to live as the mother of Christ? To be Christ's mother—it must have been a cross in itself that she bore throughout her life.

About the Author

Alban Kojima earned an M.A. in musicology from Temple University and an M.S. in information science from Drexel University in Philadelphia. For twenty-five years he held the position of Japanese Studies Informationist at the University of Pennsylvania and, at the same time, taught a graduate course entitled "Japanese Studies Resources and Problems of Research." Since late 2012, Kojima has focused on writing. He is the author of two nonfiction books published in Japanese: *Yuzo Kayama and His Music: A Global Fascination* (Tokyo: Sairyūsha, 2014); and *Alexei Sultanov* (Tokyo: Alpha Beta Books, 2017). Additionally, he published his first fiction entitled *Coal Boy* last spring (Toronto, Canada: Guernica World Editions, 2023). Kojima lives in Cherry Hill, New Jersey.

Printed by Imprimerie Gauvin
Gatineau, Québec